But You Can't Hide

LINDA FREENY

Ordering Information:

For orders and inquiries, please contact:
1-888-375-9818
www.toplinkpublishing.com
bookorder@toplinkpublishing.com

Printed in the United States of America

But You Can't Hide

Chapter One

Traffic was light. Normally Joanne would have welcomed that, but not today. Dodging cars would have been a welcome diversion from her troubled thoughts. She turned on the radio. Loud rock music blasted her ears. His love for that kind of music was David's one imperfection, and one that she'd allowed him. She switched to another frequency that played soothing ballads. It didn't help. She turned off the radio, but the silence was worse. She was uncomfortably aware of her own uneven breathing. A panic attack! Please, not now. She popped a valium into her mouth and allowed it to wash down in a sea of saliva.

She came to an intersection inviting a U-turn. She could go back, a voice of hope born out of desperation whispered. But no, she had to see this through. What else could she do? What else would make everything right again?

Finally, she reached her destination. She turned off the engine and the red Porsche went silent. David's car. It had seemed only logical to bring his car and not her own sedate Lincoln Town Car. Her heart pumped wildly as she stared over at the two-story brick building. She had never been inside a police station before. Not even...not even then. Her parents had seen to it that it wasn't necessary. They had fixed it like they'd fixed everything else in her life.

You don't have to do this, she reasoned. You can go home. No one will know that David is gone, no more than they knew he was even here. You and he led such a private life in the country. You met no one. And no one much ever met you. Even then, only tradesmen.

She filled the silence with her own voice. "You want him back, don't you? You want things to be like they were? Only, face it, you can't keep on pretending you're going to wake up in the morning and find him lying there beside you unless you do something about it."

Anger and fear caused her voice to rise. "I can't do it. I can't just walk in there and say my husband is missing, and he's been missing for months. Because sooner or later it will come out this is the second husband I've reported missing in the last nine years. And Michael, like David, left me one morning, and I never saw him again."

She stuffed her hand in her mouth and stifled a scream.

* * *

Detective Marshall Hollings wiped the sweat from his brow and brushed away a persistent mosquito. Damn this heat. Damn the fact that he felt all of his fifty-two years. And damn the fact that "blue flu" had him and every other high-ranking detective doing double duty.

He looked at the woman who sat across from his desk. She was this side of forty, her hair pulled severely back in an unbecoming bun. She had gone to great pains to make a not unattractive face, homely. Her suit was expensive and so were her accessories. The small amount of jewelry she wore was quality, a diamond encrusted wedding band, a diamond watch, and diamond stud earrings. More significant, her demeanor spelled class with a capital C. But it was her eyes that caught his immediate attention, shadowed by dark circles. She looked like she hadn't slept in days.

He yawned. Heat made him weary, and fourteen straight hours of duty wasn't helping anything.

"How long's he been missing, Ma'am?"

She turned away from him.

"It isn't a hard question, Mrs..." he looked distractedly around the room, and then down at the mound of unfinished paper work. Christ, he could use some sleep and a bath.

"Channing. Joanne Channing. And maybe it's a harder question to answer than you think. David…David has been missing for some time. For months."

Marshall let out a sigh. "It's been a long day. For a moment I thought you said he'd been gone for months."

"I did."

Marshall muttered an obscenity under his breath. "Mind telling me what the hell took you so long to report him missing?"

Tiny rivulets of perspiration beaded her forehead, and not from the heat was his guess. "David was a private person, like me. He wouldn't have wanted me to make a fuss. Not until I was sure it was the right thing to do."

Marshall loosened his tie. He stared back at her shrewdly. "It took you one hell of a long time, Lady."

"I'm here, Detective. Isn't that what's important?"

She had to choose this week, when they were operating on a skeleton force, he thought. Just his luck. "Interesting, that you use past tense. You think your husband is dead?"

"I don't know what to think."

"Really! Well you've had plenty of time to think about where he is, and what might have happened to him."

"I hoped he might come back."

The only emotion he sensed in her was a well-controlled underlying fear. What was she afraid of? "Now you don't think he will?"

"No. I mean I don't know."

Marshall settled back in his char. "So, tell me about him."

She looked surprised. "What?"

"I said tell me about him. What kind of man was he? Did he play around? Was there another woman? Did you love him? Did he love you? Did you marry him for money? That's not paste you're wearing. Tell me everything."

She jerked up out of her seat. "I don't have to take this kind of abuse. I knew it was a mistake to come here. I'll work this out for myself…somehow." She bit down on her lip, perilously close to tears.

Marshall raised himself up, towering over her scant five-feet-two frame by more than a foot. "It ain't that easy, Mrs. Channing. You can't just walk in here and announce that your husband took a hike months ago, talk like he's dead, and just walk outa here."

"Try me, Detective." Her lips quivered.

"I might just do that. Call me contrary, but I have a few questions, and, like it or not, you will answer them."

She bristled. "I don't think so." She reached into her purse and withdrew an embossed business card. Her hand was shaking. Whether it was from anger or fear he wasn't sure. He decided it was both.

"If you have any more questions," she said, "you can talk to my attorney." She handed him the card.

Marshall raised an eyebrow as he read the gold lettering.

CHARLTON HAYWARD
Attorney at Law

Marshall drew in his breath. Hayward was heavy duty. An East coast lawyer, he only dealt with the very rich or the very famous.

He gave her a look of grudging admiration. She'd thwarted his threat by trumping his king with an ace. A damned big ace at that.

"Okay. Leave me your phone number and an address." He gave her a long hard look. "You'll be hearing from me, Mrs. Channing. Count on it."

* * *

A half hour later, Captain Hal Thomas stopped by Marshall's desk. He passed a weary hand across his brow. Like Marshall, he was well into his second shift. "Good news, Marsh. Just got word the crisis is over. We'll have a full crew tomorrow. Give me the garbage files and I'll pass them on." He riffled through the stack of papers on Marshall's desk. "You sure got all the crap." He picked up Marshall's notes on Joanne Channing. "I'll give this one to Missing Persons in the morning."

Marshall retrieved the paperwork. He looked thoughtful. "No. Let me hang on to this one."

"Got a reason?"

"Just a nasty feeling this is more than it looks like on the surface. You mind?"

Thomas shrugged. "It's your call. Hey, you look beat. Take a couple of days off and let the freeloaders who had the whole week on the picket line take over."

"Thanks, Hal. Maybe I will."

Thomas laughed. "I know that look only too well. You'll be here in the morning. What are you onto, Marsh?"

"Maybe something, maybe nothing." He chuckled. "Hell, I'll probably be glad to give the Channing file to Missing Persons after I do some follow-up. It's probably just a routine skip. One more son of a bitch who got bored with his wife."

* * *

Joanne waited until she was two blocks away from the police station before she allowed herself to break down. She'd handled herself badly by using Charlie's name. Detective Hollings was no ordinary policeman. He was sharp, intuitive, and above all curious. How long before he knew everything? How long before he put two and two together and came up with five? How long before he began to openly accuse her instead of making innuendos? And of what? David wasn't dead, was he? She shivered.

She needed outside help. Someone other than the police. Maybe if David could be located before they found him he could avoid a confrontation with the past. But who could she turn to? Charlie Hayward? No. He would only tell her to play it close, and it was too late for that now.

Joanne pulled the car over to a corner phone booth. She picked up a phone book and thumbed through the yellow pages, stopping at the section that advertised private investigations. There were only five firms listed. She closed her eyes and stabbed her finger into the flimsy paper, tearing it. Her finger landed on the name T.J. McCall, leading her to a small one-eighth-of-a-page ad that stated that T.J. McCall handled insurance, domestic and miscellaneous investigations. Joanne wrote down the address, started to dial the number, and then changed her mind. She would take a chance on his being in. Joanne ripped the page from the phone book and placed it in her pocket.

* * *

The offices of T.J. McCall were on the third floor of a three-story older building in the heart of town. Joanne relaxed a little. Driving there she couldn't help thinking about the movies she'd seen about private investigators, most of the more colorful doing business from sleazy locations in small questionable quarters. T.J. McCall must be somewhat successful, she decided. The outer office was spacious and respectably furnished, and the woman sitting at a huge oak desk was middle-aged and well-dressed.

It was she who now said, "Can I help you?"

"I saw your ad in the yellow pages. I need help in finding someone. Is Mr. McCall in?"

The woman smiled as if harboring a delicious secret. "You came without an appointment?"

"Yes, I'm sorry. I came on impulse, I'm afraid." She turned to leave. "I'll call for an appointment later."

Something about Joanne captured the woman's attention. Maybe it was her look of helplessness, or her manner, that of someone with breeding. Not all of T.J.'s clients were of this high caliber.

"Have a seat," the woman said. "I think T.J. can make time for you. Wait here, I'll go see."

"No, I'll..."

"Please," the woman insisted. "I'll be right back."

Less than three minutes later the woman returned. "T.J. will see you. Please go in."

Joanne got up out of the chair nervously fingering her large leather purse. She turned the knob of the inner door and stepped inside.

The tastefully decorated interior of the room was lost on her as she met luminous green eyes of the only other inhabitant of the room. Green eyes framed by red hair that could only be natural and even white teeth in a face that could be described as mildly sensuous. The eyes, the hair, the teeth, belonged to a woman in her early thirties, impeccably dressed in a green and black Liz Claiborne suit. She was casually leaning against the corner of a mahogany and leather desk.

"Excuse me," Joanne stammered. "The woman outside said that Mr. McCall was expecting me."

The redhead extended her hand. "I doubt that Pearl said exactly that. I mean the Mr. McCall part. I'm T.J. McCall."

"But you're a woman!"

T.J. was used to this reaction, and had long ago given up defending her choice of career to clients, or anyone else for that matter. "True. Pearl said you were looking for someone," T.J. said. "Why don't you start with your name, and who you're looking for?"

Joanne sank down in a chair. "I guess it's all right. You being a woman, I mean. My name is Joanne. Joanne Channing. My husband David is missing."

"Did you think about calling the police?"

Joanne nodded. "I did. A while ago. I talked with a Detective Hollings. I suspect he believes that I had something to do with David's disappearance. You see, David has been gone for quite a while. A few months."

T.J., to her credit showed no visible reaction to the news that David Channing, gone for so long, was just now the cause for alarm in his wife's mind. "Why report him missing after all this time? Or better yet, why not report him missing sooner?"

Joanne searched T.J.'s face. Could she trust her? Should she? Should she tell her about Michael? She started to, and found that she couldn't. Not yet. Only a fool would tell everything to someone you found in the yellow pages, and a woman in a man's profession at that. "I had my reasons," she said. "For now, I'd like to keep them to myself." She reached into her purse. "I brought a picture of David with me. It's not very good; David's camera shy. It's all I have."

T.J. accepted the photo. It was slightly out of focus, but she could tell that David Sinclair was younger than his wife, blond, and boyishly good-looking.

"Did he take any of his things with him? Is his car missing?"

"He took some of his clothes, not all of them. And he took the Cadillac, though the Porsche was really his car."

"Do you have a license number?"

"Yes. Not with me, but I can call it in to you."

"Good. Leave it with Pearl."

"I should tell you that my attorney looked for him for a while, and gave up, and he had extensive connections. Personally, I don't think that David wants to be, or can be found."

T.J. frowned. "That's a strange choice of words, Mrs. Channing, yet you seem so sure of what you're saying." She placed a hand over Joanne's. "Believe me; if Marshall Hollings thinks you have something to hide, you'll play hell shaking him. He's like a dog with a bone if he thinks there's any meat on it."

"You know him?"

T.J. smiled. "Very well. He and my father were partners once. He was with my father the night he died from a bullet delivered by a crazed drug addict."

Joanne pulled her hand away. "If you and he are that close, maybe I should..."

"Go somewhere else? Go ahead. But Marshall will talk to me when he wouldn't to anyone else. The yellow pages may have led you here to me, but if that's the case, it's an opportune twist of fate. Now, are you going to stay and talk to me, or are you going to continue to sit on the edge of that chair as if it were wired for electricity?"

Joanne sighed. "I'll stay."

"Good. I'll make sure you don't regret the decision. Tell me, when did you last see your husband?"

Joanne closed her eyes. She could still see David's handsome face in her mind's eye, glistening after a marathon of lovemaking. She could still hear him saying after the third time that night, just as he always did, that you never did anything that good just once. She could still hear him saying, "I love you. Don't ever leave me." Instead, he'd been the one to leave. The next morning she'd awakened to an empty bed.

"I'm not sure of the date, but it was several months ago. He was gone when I woke up. At first, I thought he'd gone for a walk. He did that sometimes. But he never came back."

A woman's husband disappears and she didn't know the date? Most women would have had the date committed to memory, like a birthday! T.J. almost started to ask all the routine questions, like was there another woman, had they been happy, but she resisted the impulse. The woman barely trusted her now, and Marshall would have asked her all those same questions anyway. "I'll get right on it, Mrs. Channing. It would help if you could remember the exact date he disappeared."

Joanne's expression was one of gratitude. She'd seen those awful questions poised on T.J.'s lips. "I'll try, and thank you." She turned to leave, and then pivoted around. "What does T.J. stand for?"

T.J. grinned. "Theresa Jane. From the time I could first pronounce it, I hated it. My father called me T.J. as compensation for my not being the son he wanted. I had my name legally changed years ago."

"So that you could pass as a man if you had to?"

The smile faded. "No. Never felt the need. Besides, Theresa sounds like a saint. The smile came back. "Whatever else you hear or learn about me, Mrs. Channing, it won't be that! Oh, and please leave your contact information with Pearl before you leave"

* * *

Marshall Hollings looked up at T.J. and smiled. T.J. had her father's courage and recklessness, her mother's beauty, and an inborn sense of integrity she'd acquired from both. He was as fond of her as he was of his own two daughters. Fonder, maybe in some respects. "Long time no see, T.J. What makes me think that you're coming here today isn't just because you've missed me?"

She reached over and hugged him, oblivious of the envious glances of several other men in the smoke-filled squad room. "I hate it when you're so damn smart," she said. "And I have missed you."

Marshall reached for a cigarette ignoring her frown. T.J. had preached the evils of smoking to him and her father since she was in kindergarten. Said it would kill them. But a bullet, not nicotine had killed Clint McCall, and Marshall was still around. So, his lungs hurt once in a while. So what? "Still seeing that guy? What's his name? Scott?"

"You know damn well his name is Scott. You also know we live together. And yes, we're making it work."

"Why don't you marry him?"

It was the same question Scott asked her at least once a week. "I've been married, Marsh. It's not all it's cracked up to be."

"And it ain't all bad. And they ain't all like Jim, either."

"Thank God for that. And I didn't come here to discuss my personal life. I came here about Joanne Channing."

Marshall blew out smoke and watched it form a circle. "What does she have to do with you?"

"She's my client, Marsh. She thinks you suspect her of something dastardly in her husband's disappearance."

He ground out his cigarette. "It's possible. What did she hire you to do?"

"Same thing she asked of you. She wants me to find him." She grinned. "You could make it easy on a girl and tell me what, if anything, you've turned up."

"Or I could make it real easy and tell you to walk away from this one. There's something strange about the woman. Something I can't put my finger on. For openers, she threw Charlton Hayward at me when I started to ask her questions she didn't like, and she's frightened of something."

"THE Charlton Hayward?"

"The same. I called his office. They claim to have never heard of Joanne Channing. I ran a make on her and neither she nor her husband existed until they showed up in these parts two years ago." He stroked his chin. "I sure could use a set of prints. The only way I can get them legitimately is to pull her in, but I don't have cause...yet. I don't suppose..."

"No!" And I can't believe you even asked. She's my client for Christ's sake!"

"Then tell me, who the hell is she?"

T.J. leaned forward. "I thought I was the one looking for information. All I know is that she's a troubled woman, and, if she's frightened, it's probably you who scared her, you big bully." The affection in her voice belied the harshness of her words.

"I learned a long time ago that you can't scare someone who doesn't have anything to hide. When you find out who she really is, you will call me?"

T.J. grinned. "You know the rules, Marsh. If she says I can, I will. That's the best I can do. Besides, you'll probably have the answer to that before I do. You have a whole police force at your disposal. All I have is Pearl."

"Fair enough. But having Pearl is like having an entire police force." Marshall shook his head. "Why didn't you become a lawyer, T.J.? Your parents always hoped you would?"

"I know what my parents hoped for. But more than that they wanted me to be happy. I went to law school, passed the bar, even married an attorney, if you recall. That's when I got an inside look at what most of them are like. I decided I didn't want any part of that inner circle. Besides, I like what I do." She gently shrugged her shoulders and smiled. "And someone has to act as a buffer between people like Joanne Channing and tough guys like you."

"You're too young to be this bitter, T.J. Like I said, they ain't all like Jim."

A frown creased her forehead. "Unfortunately, too many of them are. I'll be seeing you, Marsh."

"A lot, I think," he added ruefully as she turned to leave. "A hell of a lot if you insist on keeping the Channing woman as a client."

Chapter Two

T.J. called Pearl from her cell phone. "I just saw Marsh," she said. Apparently, our new client isn't using her real name. There has to be a reason. Check the records and see who owned the land that Joanne Channing and her husband built the house on. Then, find out if they bought it direct, or went through a real estate agent. Find out if they paid cash, and if so, what bank the funds were drawn on."

"Anything else?" Pearl responded with a trace of gentle sarcasm in her voice.

T.J. smiled. Pearl was a whiz on a computer, and great on the phone, but that didn't mean she liked stationary leg work. "No. Call Gregg. Looks like I may need him to beat the bushes after you've driven the skeletons out from underneath them."

Gregg Brooks was a free lance investigator who worked for several attorneys. T.J. was his only private investigator client. T.J. claimed it was because she paid him exorbitant fees. Pearl, however, maintained it was because he had a "thing" for T.J.

"I'll call him. Where can I find you?"

"Home. This could be a long case, or at best a complicated one, and that means lots of hours away from home. I'll need to soothe the savage beast I live with."

Pearl laughed. "Hardly a proper adjective. The only savage thing about Scott is the way he feels about you, and what you do for a living."

* * *

When T.J. arrived home, Scott's car was in the driveway. She felt the hood. It was still warm so he hadn't been home long. She sighed. She cared deeply for Scott Newton. More than she'd cared for any man she'd ever known. She was terrified of losing him, but not nearly as terrified as she was of marrying him.

She had loved Jim Westfield, too, and more importantly, liked him once. Those emotions had ended when they'd sealed their union with a marriage certificate at almost the same time he'd emerged as a successful criminal law attorney. That alone might have not driven them apart, but his using his office like a studio casting couch, had. And now, more often than she'd like, her relationship with Scott was fraught with minefields because of her work, and her refusal to legitimize their relationship.

A psychologist, Scott had no burning ambitions to conquer the medical world, a quality T.J. not only admired, but appreciated. And he had no major hang-ups, not unless you counted T.J. herself.

He'd heard her drive up. By the time she entered the kitchen of the suburban home they shared, the only asset she'd kept from her marriage to Jim, he had a drink waiting for her.

Scott was almost criminally good-looking, but seemed to be blissfully unaware of how attractive he was. He was thirty-five, never married, and claimed he'd die a bachelor if T.J. kept turning down his proposal of marriage.

She took his drink from him and kissed him gently on the lips. "Thanks."

"New case?" He queried.

"You've been talking to Pearl," she accused.

He kissed the tip of her lightly freckled nose. "No, but you always give yourself away."

"How?"

"Never mind. A guy has to have some secrets. You do have a new case?"

She took a sip of her drink. "Mmm. A woman wants me to find her missing husband. He's been gone for months, and she's just now reporting him officially missing."

"Months?"

"Yes. And she's lying about who she is. Which means she could be lying about everything else? Marsh thinks she may be covering up her husband's murder."

"He said that!"

"Not in so many words. But I know Marsh, and how he thinks."

Scott placed his drink on the counter. "That works both ways, T.J. He knows you pretty well, too."

"He thinks I should drop the case."

"Maybe you should."

She shook her finger at him. "Not fair. I don't play private detective when I come home, you shouldn't play psychologist."

"But you do bring your work home. Look at you now! You're milking me, T.J. I don't mind, but at least give me equal time."

She stroked his cheek. "You're right. I guess I was looking for reasons to stay on the case when every instinct tells me to pull out now."

"Instinct or Marsh?"

She smiled. "Sometimes I think they're the same thing. Are you, hungry?"

"Not for food." He pulled her to him. "I had something else in mind."

T.J. grinned. "I was hoping you would." She grabbed him by his tie and led him down the hall to the bedroom.

* * *

"Any progress?" T.J. asked as she breezed through the door of her offices at a few minutes after nine.

"Funny you should ask," Pearl quipped.

T.J. suppressed a smile. "It's going to be one of those days, is it? Well, let me get a cup of coffee and then come on into my office and enlighten me."

Pearl had her notebook and several pages of computer read-outs ready when she entered the room. She took a seat across from

T.J. "Joanne Channing didn't buy the land the house was built on from anyone. Kirkland Industries owns the land and the house too. Or they did until a few months back when Kirkland Enterprises deeded half the property to David Sinclair."

T.J. leaned forward in her chair, almost spilling her coffee. David Channing?"

Pearl nodded. "Looks like."

"Which makes Joanne, not Joanne Channing, but Joanne Sinclair?"

"Try Joanne Kirkland, and she is Kirkland Enterprises. I had Joanne Kirkland's picture faxed across. It's the same woman who came to your office."

"Did you get background on Joanne Kirkland?"

"Give a girl a chance. It's coming." Pearl checked her watch. "Should have the info in about an hour."

T.J. stood. She paced the plush carpet. "Marsh is too smart not to have gone the same route we did. My guess is he knows as much as we do right now. It doesn't look good for Joanne unless she has a sound reason for disguising her real identity. An hour, you said? Call Joanne and tell her I'll see her at noon. She has some explaining to do."

* * *

Joanne's house resembled a hunting lodge, built of wood and stone, a one-level structure that cost more than three hundred-dollars a square foot to build. While some of it was natural, the landscaping included a small forest of imported full-grown pine and spruce trees that gave the dwelling a fortress-like privacy. The setting was a mirage in an otherwise scrub brush strewn landscape. Situated on forty acres, the nearest house was a quarter-mile away; sheer cliffs and the ocean a scant ten miles off.

If she hadn't known the house was here, she'd have missed it and driven right by it, T.J. thought as she parked her car in the gravel driveway.

Joanne peered out the window. When she saw it was T.J., she hurried to open the door. "Have you found out anything? Any leads on David?"

"Little chance of that on the skimpy and misleading information you gave me. We need to talk, Mrs. Sinclair."

Joanne started. "You know who I am!"

"It's what I do."

"I see. I should be impressed, and I am. Please come in."

Seated in the living room, T.J. pulled a folder from her briefcase. Once again she was reminded of a lodge. A huge stone fireplace covered one whole side of the room, and the walls were polished cedar. "Before you became Mrs. Sinclair, Mrs. David Sinclair, that is, you were Mrs. Michael Sinclair, and before that, you were Joanne Kirkland, heiress to the Kirkland billions. You want to tell me why the need for the charade? And why you came to this out of the way locale and started calling yourself Joanne Channing?"

Joanne stared past T.J. "Why don't you tell me what you know about me, instead?"

"All right. David Sinclair is your second husband. You were married to a Michael Sinclair previously. David, I assume, is his brother or a close relative."

"His brother."

"All right. His brother. You were married to Michael Sinclair for two years when he disappeared in a boating accident. All that was ever found on the lake was an empty vessel. No body was ever recovered. Since the lake was icy all year round, and very deep, it's possible for a body to never surface. Now, you've reported David missing. It doesn't look good for you. In fact, I'm surprised Detective Hollings hasn't come banging on your door."

"You told him about me!"

"Give me credit for integrity, Joanne. Of course I didn't tell him. But Marsh is an intelligent resourceful cop. If I can trace your background, so can he."

"I didn't kill David."

"But you think he's dead?"

Tears rushed to Joanne's eyes. T.J. looked away. A woman's tears always reminded her of her own vulnerability.

"If he isn't," Joanne whispered. "Then where is he? He knows what I went though after Michael drowned. He knows how I endured all those terrible accusing questions. He wouldn't have wanted me to go through it again, and alone."

"Are you sure?"

Doubt crossed Joanne's face. "I think so. I married Michael because I was sure no one else would ever ask me. It was different with David. I wasn't looking for romance, but I fell in love. I fell in love with the idea of him long before I knew I loved him. And he loved me," she added defiantly. "I know he did."

T.J. referred back to her file. "When you were fifteen you were sent to a boarding school in England. I don't know what happened there, but you were brought back to the States, and you spent the next three years in a sanitarium, admitted for a nervous breakdown. You were home from the sanitarium only a year when your parents died in a car crash. Not much is known after that until you married Michael Sinclair thirteen years later." She placed the file on her lap and tapped it with her fingers. "But all this is…are words. Nothing in this report tells me how you felt, what really happened at that boarding school, and what you're so afraid of now."

Joanne clenched her hands into a tight ball. "Maybe I'm afraid of going mad, Miss McCall. Maybe, just maybe, it's no more complicated than that."

Her fists unclenched, and for a moment, she looked almost serene as she stared back at T.J.'s open-mouthed gape.

* * *

Pearl looked up in anticipation as T.J. entered the office. "How'd it go? Do we still have a client?"

T.J. thought about how her conversation with Joanne had continued after Joanne's astounding remark about being afraid of going mad. She claimed to have blocked out the event or events that had led to her internment in an institution.

"It's true," Joanne had said. "I don't remember anything. The first thing I can recall after it happened, whatever it was, was waking up in that institution. Oh, it was the best that money could buy, made to look like a resort instead of a mental hospital." She shuddered. "But, the smell. I never will forget the smell. Antiseptic, pine cleaners, the smell of sick people. Did you know places like that and everyone in them put out an odor of their own?" She shuddered once more. "I still take four showers a day because I'm afraid of ever smelling like that again."

"Did you believe her?" Pearl asked.

"Maybe. I told her the only way I'd stay on the case was if she understood that there were to be no restrictions. I warned her that if I was to continue looking for David Sinclair, nothing or no one was sacred. And, that if it meant investigating her past, I wanted a free hand to do it."

Pearl learned forward. "And?"

"It was touch and go for a few seconds, then she gave me carte blanche, not only with her past, but she gave me an open check book. Charlton Hayward really is her attorney, by the way. He's been representing the family since before she was born. Joanne is clearing the way for me to talk to him. He probably knows more about Kirkland Enterprises than anyone."

"That's where you're headed?"

"Yes."

"Then, what?"

"A trip to London to the boarding school where Joanne suffered some kind of trauma, and a visit to the Connecticut institution where Joanne stayed for three years."

"Which one of these exotic journeys is mine?" A voice intervened. "Personally, I vote for the trip to England."

The two women turned to stare at the intruder. T.J. smiled fondly at him. Gregg Brooks was like the brother she never had. He was carelessly good-looking, his too long hair touching his collar.

Young, but not impulsive, T.J. considered him the best in his field. She'd tried to get him to join her organization permanently, but he liked his freedom. She respected that, because in so many ways they were alike. Only their reasons were different. Pearl had briefed Gregg earlier about the case.

"Sorry, Gregg," she responded. "It's the nut house for you, and anyone who may have known Joanne Kirkland well. When I get back from England we'll join forces and try to trace David Sinclair's last moves."

"The cart before the horse?" he said.

"I don't think so," T.J. said. "I think the more we know about Joanne, the easier it will be to find her husband."

Gregg was pessimistic. "Assuming he's still alive. Why don't you just ask the lady what you want to know about her?" He paused. "I see by your grimace that the lady wants us to do it the hard way. So be it." He grinned. "Besides, when the hell was it ever easy?"

* * *

Scott handed T.J. a stack of blouses and watched her pack them neatly in her suitcase. "Last chance this week to marry me and let me take you away from all this."

T.J. stopped what she was doing and kissed him. "No, but thanks for asking."

"What if I stopped asking?"

She stepped back from him. "Would you do that?"

"Would it matter to you?"

It surprised her just how much, and she knew it was both contrary and unfair of her to feel this way. "A lot. I love you, Scott, and you know that, I just can't..."

He placed his fingers on her lips. "It's okay. I'm a patient and a stubborn man."

She sighed in relief. "Thanks. Maybe someday when..."

"I said, I can wait." There was an edge to his voice. "Oh, and I forgot to tell you, Jim called here earlier."

An angry flush spread over her face showcasing scattered freckles. "What about?"

"He said he was getting audited, and you had all the records. He wanted to stop by and look through canceled checks from three years ago."

"To hell with him! Anyway, I think I tossed him."

Scott stroked her cheek. "I doubt it. You never throw anything away."

T.J. pushed him away from her. "I said to hell with him. Who does he think he is that he can announce that he's stopping by like he still lives here?"

"Give him some slack, T.J. The break-up was as hard on him as it was on you. Worse really. The divorce was your idea."

"What was I supposed to do? Wait until he got tired of sleeping with every female client that walked through his door? And I don't want to talk about him."

"Maybe you'd feel better if you did."

"And maybe I'd feel better if you kept your nose out of it. I'm not one of your patients, Scott. I don't need counseling."

"Okay." But he was hurt.

Damn. She'd done it again. Reacted without thinking. "Sorry, Scott. Don't let Jim come between us," she pleaded. "He screwed up my past; I won't let him jeopardize my future. Besides, it's our last night together for a while."

He drew her to him. He kissed her, his tongue seeking hers. His teeth nibbled at her ear. "You're a hard one not to want to analyze. I never met anyone like you. You're beautiful, stubborn, fearless, yet the most vulnerable human being I know. Outside, you're tough, ready to take on all comers, a worthy opponent for the male counterparts who do what you do for a living. Inside, you're fire, and you're ice, and you're Jello and you're putty."

She pulled away from him a troubled look on her face. "Sometimes it's frightening just how well you know me."

* * *

The jumbo jet was ten minutes outside New York. T.J. had called ahead to Hayward and he was sending someone to meet her. Not because he considered her important, she knew, but because the Kirkland billions were.

The man who met her was in his late twenties. A would-be lawyer, she suspected but an obvious office flunkie.

The man took her suitcase from her. "I'm Roger Casey, one of Mr. Hayward's paralegals. He said to get you set up in a hotel, and he'll see you in the morning."

"Tell me, Roger. It is okay to call you, Roger?"

He nodded. "Of, course."

"Charlton Hayward comes with a heady reputation. What's he really like, I mean the man, not the lawyer."

Roger smiled. "I never made that distinction. Charlton Hayward is Charlton Hayward inside and outside the courtroom. Anyway, I'm only a paralegal. I'm not privileged to know anything about the man on a personal level."

T.J. admitted to more than just curiosity where Charlton Hayward was concerned. To someone who had passed the bar and considered, however briefly, a career practicing law, meeting Hayward was tantamount to meeting God.

Chapter Three

Charlton Hayward's offices took up the entire floor of a luxury Fifth Avenue building, which came as no real surprise to T.J. She would have expected nothing less of him. Nor was she surprised when she was subjected to a half-hour wait beyond the time scheduled for their meeting.

Hayward's private office was a showcase of exquisite art, priceless antiques, and carpeting so plush it threatened to swallow her ankles. Instead of being a vulgar display of wealth, as it could so easily have been, it was merely a gracious symbol of well-earned success. Damn few people, out loud anyway, begrudged this man his lofty position in the legal profession, or the wealth he'd acquired along the way.

Charlton Hayward was in his early sixties. He'd never married. He had thick silver-gray hair and a moustache to match. He was trim, and despite his years, was one of the most striking men T.J. had ever met. Steel blue eyes locked with hers as he extended his hand. When T.J. took it, his grip was firm.

"So, you're the person Joanne has put so much faith in." His voice was richly timbered, deep and authoritative. "I hope you're worthy of that faith."

T.J. flushed. His last words were a clear warning. T.J. felt like a school girl. She voiced her thoughts out loud. "Give me a minute to adjust, will you? I first saw you when you gave a lecture when I was attending law school. You overwhelmed me then, and you're doing it now, and I don't think that's solid ground for either of us, not if we want to help my client."

"Well said. Why'd you quit law school?"

"You assume I did, or worse, that I flunked out."

Hayward placed his fingers together and cupped them under his chin. "Touché. What happened?"

"I passed the bar, but didn't choose to practice law." Her tone was defensive, and she hated herself for the lapse.

His knowing smile told her that he not only knew he'd scored a hit, but was pleased about it. "Well, it's a free country. Tell me, why private investigations?"

She wasn't about to let him have another shot at her. "My father was a cop, a damned good one. I toyed with the idea of following in his footsteps, especially after he died, but I didn't like the rigid discipline or the frustration of picking up bad guys and having men like you and my ex-husband get them off. I worked for the D.A.'s office for two years as an investigator. I didn't like that job either. All I was doing, I realized, was trading one unsatisfactory profession for another. I was helping to find evidence to put the guilty away, good solid unshakable evidence, by the way, and still guys like you either got the bad guys off, or got them sentences that were a mere slap on the wrist. I discovered that I liked the investigating process. It's like reading a book and not knowing the ending until the last page." She flushed. "It occurred to me that I'm answering all the questions, and I came here to get answers from you."

He smiled again, but this time the gesture seemed more genuine. "Of course. What exactly do you want to know?"

"Everything about Joanne and everything you know about her husbands. She's reluctant to talk about herself, or them, but is willing to let you do it. Why?"

"You come straight to the point. I like that. See, you're not intimidated by me at all."

"That was a long time ago."

"He went on. "Joanne wouldn't want to talk about herself because she's a terribly unsure person. You'd have to have known how it was to be raised in the Kirkland household to appreciate that. The Kirkland's had a son. He died as a result of leukemia at the age of sixteen. Joanne was ten at the time and her parent didn't know what to do with her. Their life had revolved around their only son and heir. Add to that the fact that Joanne was a quiet, not particularly attractive child at the time. She'd lived so long in her brother's shadow she was as lost as her parents were after he died. Eventually, they shipped her off to England to a boarding school."

"Where something happened," T.J. said. "Do you know what it was?"

He shook his head. "Her parents refused to talk about it. It's possible only Joanne knows for sure. If that's true, it's locked away securely in her subconscious. Years of therapy proved that."

"Is Joanne a stable person?" T.J. asked.

Hayward gave her a long hard look. "Joanne has had her problems. She's been known to black out on rare occasions, but, in spite of all that, she is in charge of herself, and certainly not insane. I'd stake my law practice on that."

It was a dramatic and seemingly sincere statement, one that T.J. was convinced he hadn't made lightly. "I had to ask."

"Certainly." He checked his watch, a trinket that cost a year's salary for most people. "It's getting late. Why don't we finish this conversation over dinner? You can relax away from these official surroundings and start looking at me as a human being. I am, you know. Human, I mean."

She hadn't fooled him a bit. She was still intimidated by him, if only a little. She had a ridiculous image of butterflies escaping her stomach and flying all over the room. She recovered. "I'd be happy to have dinner with you."

"Wonderful. I like you, Miss McCall. And I, for one, look forward to this evening. It's not every day that I can walk in Twenty-One with a woman as attractive as you on my arm."

"Twenty-one?"

"Yes, any objections?"

He mind raced. She felt lightheaded. Had she brought anything to wear that would be remotely appropriate? Oh, to hell with it! She'd blow the budget and buy a new dress.

* * *

T.J., resplendent in a floor-length metallic silver dress with a scooped cowl neckline and split up one side that reached her knee, tried not to look as overwhelmed as she felt.

The Twenty-One Club! Wait until she told Pearl!

Hayward wore a white jacket and black pants that looked great on him. He looked ten years younger than he had earlier today. Of course, the soft lighting helped, but a closer look revealed an almost invisible trace of make-up around his eyes and jowl. T.J. smiled inwardly. The man was human. Charlton Hayward feared the sands of time just like everyone else.

He'd ordered a bottle of Don Perignon, 1969 and the waiter poured them each a glass after allowing Hayward to test the contents of the bottle first. After pronouncing it excellent, he raised his glass to hers. "To your first trip to New York."

"Is it that obvious?"

He smiled. "Only to a native."

"Do you dine here often?" She asked. "Or are you trying to impress me?"

She wished she could take back the words. What a stupid thing to say! Hayward didn't need to impress anyone, least of all her. She looked around the room, spotted a well-known movie star, started to point him out, and abruptly changed her mind. Get it together, T.J., she warned herself. You're acting like a country hick. "Tell me about Joanne's first husband. Where did she meet him?"

The waiter appeared and asked if they were ready to order. Hayward ordered for both of them. "I hope you don't mind?"

"Not at all. It's probably best. Personally, I'm a steak, hamburger and hot dog junkie myself. My palate doesn't have much class."

"But you do, my dear, and you have a charming and disarming habit of pretending not to." He sighed. "Ah yes, Michael. Michael entered Joanne's life through the art medium. They attended the same classes. Joanne, mistakenly so, thought she had nothing to offer a man. Her self-esteem was poor, and when Michael asked her to marry him, she jumped at the chance. They were marred before I could caution her."

"He married her for her money?"

"Yes, but the joke was on him. Joanne's parents left everything to her in a life estate. She had, and still has no power to will her assets to anyone."

"You told him this?"

"Yes. They were married only a few months when Joanne had a nasty, suspicious accident. She was found at the base of the long winding staircase of the Kirkland Connecticut mansion. I confronted Michael with my suspicions, and told him why it would do him no good to rid himself of Joanne."

"How did he take it?"

"Very well. He was an excellent actor. In fact, he had been one once, among other things, in a mediocre way for several years. He was careful after that. Joanne was extremely generous. He lacked for nothing. Her parent's will allowed for her to spend money as she wished, even put property in her husband's name, should she marry, as long as the value of that interest didn't exceed seven hundred and fifty thousand dollars. The boat that he took out on the day he died was a gift from her."

"What happens to everything if Joanne dies?"

"There are various benefactors. Charities and institutions for the most part. The Kirkland's had no living relatives other than Joanne."

"And, David?"

He seemed to weigh his word carefully. "David was different. He was everything Joanne had deluded herself into thinking that Michael was and she needed that difference."

T.J. leaned back as the waiter placed the first course in front of her. "I don't think I'm being paranoid when I say that like Joanne, you talk about David as if he's dead."

"Quite so. Joanne thinks that he is. I tend to believe her. David would never have disappeared unless there was provocation." He frowned. "If in the end she intended to report him missing she should have told me about it."

"If she intended to report him missing?"

"It was not a careless statement, Miss McCall. After all, there was the episode with Michael."

"And you conveyed your thoughts on the matter to Joanne?"

"Of course. But, in retrospect, I don't think she would have listened to me even if I had gotten to her sooner."

"Why not?"

He sighed. "For the same reason she changed her name and traveled across the country to establish a new life. She didn't need notoriety. She needed to be left alone. There was so much notoriety when Michael drowned. David was Michael's brother, after all. Imagine, if you will, what the scandal magazines would have done with that piece of information. When she decided that she and David should be married I was easily persuaded that she... they, needed and deserved a fresh start. Kirkland Enterprises had purchased the land the house is on years ago as in investment. It was I, in fact, who suggested the location. Now, I feel responsible." He shrugged. "It seemed like a perfect plan at the time."

"Until David disappeared."

"Yes. Tell me, Miss McCall what is..."

"Please," she cautioned him. "Please don't ask me what a woman like me is doing in this line of work. I thought we addressed that question earlier."

"I wasn't going to. I'll assume you're capable until you prove otherwise. I was about to ask you what your next move is?"

"Sorry. It's a sore point with me. I'm gong to England to see if I can find out what happened to Joanne there?"

"Whatever for?"

"Because, a case like this one, with a central figure as interesting and as a guarded as Joanne is, is like a giant puzzle. In order to solve it, I have to have all the pieces, even if some of those pieces turn out to be nothing more than blue sky."

"I see. I'll call the boarding school and tell them to expect you. A word from me will gain you easy access."

No doubt, she thought.

"Thank you."

"It's the least I can do. How's your meal?"

Truthfully, she had been so absorbed with him and her surroundings; she hadn't tasted much of anything. "It was terrific. Thank you for bringing me here."

"My pleasure."

Hayward insisted on taking her to the airport himself the next day, ignoring her protests. "Nonsense. I promised Joanne I'd treat you like royalty."

He was a model of chivalry. He checked her in at British Airways desk and selected a window seat for her in first class. "I was booked on coach!" She protested.

"An uncivilized way to fly, Miss McCall. Joanne would want you to travel in comfort."

"She's more than just a client to you, isn't she?"

"Guilty. I'm fond of Joanne. Hers hasn't been an easy life in spite of the trimmings that only wealth like the Kirkland billions can give you." He frowned. "I suppose that Joanne could use your kind of services, but don't become frustrated if you fail. I couldn't bring David back into her life."

"Hopefully, I'll be luckier."

"Luck has nothing to do with it, my dear. What Joanne could really use however, is a friend. You could be that friend, Miss McCall."

T.J. shook her head. "Sorry. Befriending her would make me lose objectivity."

"You think that Joanne had something to do with David's disappearance?"

She retrieved her cosmetic case that he'd been carrying for her. "Let's just say I haven't ruled it out."

"Shouldn't you be looking for David instead of looking into Joanne's past? What can you hope to find there anyway?"

She thought she'd answered that question. He was being a typical lawyer she concluded. Don't ask the question once, but twice, or even three times, because oftentimes the answers varied enough to be significant. "I'm looking for explanations as to why two men disappeared from Joanne's life. The more I know about the lady herself, the more I'll understand the men in her life."

"Michael didn't disappear. He drowned."

"So it would seem. But there was no body."

He showed annoyance. "Take my advice, Miss McCall, don't look for something that isn't there."

"You could be right. I won't know that until I turn over all the rocks, now will I, Mr. Hayward?"

* * *

The jet to London was steeply ascending when it occurred to T.J. that in spite of his apparent openness, she really hadn't learned anything of real value from Charlton Hayward.

The mark of a great lawyer, she conceded. They never gave as much as they received, but left you thinking, at least for a while, that you'd received your moneys worth.

The jumbo jet leveled out. T.J. let out a long breath. She hated take-offs and landings. She tilted her seat backward and rested her head on the padded headrest. Hopefully, her trip to England would bear more fruit than her trip to New York.

Chapter Four

T.J. unbuckled her seat belt and looked around her and stretched. First class was almost empty. She could use a drink. Anytime she was this far off the ground, alcohol seemed like a necessary evil. She made her way up the winding staircase that led to the first class lounge. Almost immediately, a stewardess was at her side asking what she could bring her.

She was alone in the lounge when another passenger came in. Observing people was a result of her natural curiosity and an instinctive reflex that T.J. had acquired along with her work. The new arrival was tall with dark curly hair, a moustache, and a thick black beard. He looked to be in his thirties, with the most piercing blue eyes she had ever seen. Too blue to be real. Her guess would be that he wore colored contact lenses, and that his eyes were either grey or green, or maybe even a more realistic shade of blue to match his complexion.

He started to seat himself away from her, and then hesitated. "We seem to be alone up here." He smiled and indicated the empty seat next to her. "Would you mind?"

Truthfully, she welcomed the company. It would take her mind off flying. Her father had said it was the only thing that T.J. was really afraid of, but that wasn't true. She was afraid of a lot of things. Things like commitment.

"Okay if I sit here?" the man repeated.

"Of course. Sorry, I was somewhere else."

He smiled again. He had great teeth. "I noticed. First trip to London?"

"Yes. And, you?"

"No. I make regular business trips back and forth. If you need a guide...?" He grinned. "That was presumptuous. Somebody is probably meeting you in London."

"No, but thanks. Who knows, I may take you up on it."

"I'll keep my fingers crossed." He extended his hand. "My name is Mark Sanders."

She accepted his hand. It was a big strong hand, she noted, thinking that there was something else she should also store to memory. She shook her head as if to clear it. Curse this tin can with wings. It dulled her normally astute powers of observation.

"Something wrong?" he asked.

"No. I just don't like being this far off the ground. It turns me into an airhead. I don't think that mortals were meant to fly. If we were, God would have given us wings. By the way, my name is T.J. McCall."

"T.J.?"

"Yes. And don't ask me what it stands for."

He held up his hands. "You have my word." A grin lighted up his face. "Just one guess though. Thelma Jean?"

His grin was infectious. He would be an easy man to like... like a lot, if it weren't for Scott. She was suddenly overwhelmingly grateful that Scott was in her life.

"Close," she responded. "And you've had your one guess. What do you do for a living?"

"Traveling salesman." He laughed out loud. "Couldn't help myself. Actually, I'm in public relations. I free-lance for several British and American based companies. And, you?"

"I invade people's privacy." She smiled. "Sorry, but turnabout is fair play. I'm a private investigator."

"Sounds interesting. What do you investigate, and for whom?"

"Anything interesting and I work for myself. Or, others really. They hire me to come up with answers."

"Do you?"

"Most of the time."

The aircraft hit an air pocket and fell a few hundred feet. T.J. turned white as she gripped the side of her seat. "Are we going to crash?"

The movement hadn't even shaken him. "I doubt it. If we were, one of those uniformed beauties would have come rushing to our aid with pillows or something. Relax."

"Easy for you to say." T.J. stared into her empty glass at the precise moment that a stewardess appeared at her elbow with a fresh drink.

"Nothing to worry about, Miss," the stewardess said. "Can I get you something else?"

T.J. gave her a sheepish grin. "Yes. Knockout drops until we land."

Mark became her unofficial guardian until the plane finally made its descent into Heathrow airport. He offered to go with her to her hotel outside of Grosvenor Square. T.J. declined. "I have work to do, and so do you."

"Dinner, tonight?"

She was sorely tempted. She was alone in London and knew no one. But Mark would be a distraction, and a dangerous one she reflected without knowing why that thought had leaped to mind. He was charming, that was for sure, but that wasn't it. It was something else. "Thanks, but I need to get an early start tomorrow. As much as I'd like to treat this like a vacation, it isn't. When my investigation is completed I'll be heading back home."

"You're a hard woman, T.J. McCall. Can I look you up in the States?"

"No." Her tone was resolute. I'm involved with someone, Mark. Someone I care very much about. I wouldn't want to do anything to jeopardize that relationship."

He gave her a rueful smile. "I've been around enough women to know when they mean what they say. Shame." He touched her lips lightly with his own. "Maybe we'll meet again, anyway."

And with that he was gone.

* * *

It was raining. T.J. stared out her hotel window. She'd always wanted to see London. She could take an extra day at her own expense and see a few of the more famous sights. She sighed. That wouldn't be fair. She was here on business. Besides, if she was going to play hooky, it would have made sense to have had a guide like Mark. She frowned. He was charming. Probably a knock-out under that beard. So what was it about him that bothered her? She shrugged. That was the problem with her line of work. You took no one on faith. It was a wonder that she and Scott had made it this far in their relationship. More of a wonder that they'd gotten together at all.

The phone on the dresser beside her bed rang. For a dangerous second she hoped it was Mark.

It was Pearl. "How was your flight?" she asked.

"Uneventful, thank God, except for some minor turbulence."

She could almost see Pearl's grin. "Which would translate to major trouble for you, knowing how you hate to fly? You should have let Gregg go to London."

"Maybe. But I had to fly to New York, anyway. Besides, it's time I got over my fear of flying."

"It's still your mother, isn't it?"

T.J.'s mother had died in a plane crash on a visit to her family in the mid-west. It was a messy fiery crash that charred the remains of the victims so badly that none of them resembled human beings. Rachel McCall had been buried in a closed casket. "Let's say it doesn't help that she died that way. What's up?"

"Bad news. Marshall paid a visit to your client. He knows who she is. According to Joanne he gave her the third degree."

T.J. smiled. "Knowing Marsh, I understand how Joanne could interpret it that way. I'm only surprised he didn't go to see her earlier."

"He called here. He's upset with you, T.J. He said you two had a deal. "

"I didn't violate it. I told him I'd tell him Joanne's true identity if she gave her permission. She never gave it. Did you tell him where I was?"

"Only that you were out of town."

"Good. I'll visit the boarding school in the morning, find out what I can, and catch a flight back the day after."

"How did it go with Hayward?"

T.J. laughed. "He played me like a violin."

"Then he was no help?"

"Some. He got me an introduction to the head of the boarding school, and he's paving the way for Gregg at the sanitarium."

"Well, that's something, anyway. I'll see you in two days then?"

It was still raining the next morning. T.J. was supplied an umbrella by the hotel manager. The building was old, but elegant, and the wallpaper, though tasteful, had seen better days, and the building had character that T.J. appreciated.

She took a series of three buses to get to Putney where the boarding school was located. She could have taken a taxi, or a train, but she decided she'd see more of the country this way, a small but harmless diversion she rationalized. Putney was in a suburb outside of London, one of many endless small towns that ran together making it difficult to know when you'd left one and entered another.

The English, a hardy breed, filled the streets despite the rain. A sea of umbrellas created a colorful tableau. Women with shopping bags and headscarves mingled with men in caps and raincoats. Children in galoshes and plastic hats held tightly to their mother's hands.

The double-deckered red buses that she rode all had a cheerful conductor on board, who punched tickets and walked the aisles with a warm smile. She felt an instant affinity with the English commoner. She really must come back here with Scott. They'd never taken a real vacation together. The closest to it they'd come was a weekend in Las Vegas.

The bus dropped her a few yards from the school. Here she encountered a different, starker view of England. A six-foot brick wall covered with ivy surrounded the grounds. A tree-lined drive led to an imposing granite structure of indeterminate age. Walking to the entrance T.J. couldn't help comparing it to Alcatraz. Joanne had spent years here! T.J. shuddered.

Classes were in session. T.J.'s high heeled pumps echoed in the wide hallway. She looked around for someone, anyone, to tell her where to find the head mistress. There was no one, only muted sounds from the closed doors of the classrooms. She stared at the empty hall. She began to turn around and head back when a hand was placed on her shoulder. She stared. A woman who looked to be in her seventies stood behind her.

"I'm Miss Bramfield," the woman rasped. "Head mistress, here. You must be Miss McCall. Americans are so dreadfully easy to spot. My office is down the hall. Please follow me."

Joanne had been sent here! What was her parents thinking? This woman looked as warm as the granite exterior of the building.

Miss Bramfield's office was functional. A desk with two chairs in front and several filing cabinets were the only furnishings, except for some pictures on the wall of several rather grim-looking people.

Miss Bramfield followed T.J.'s gaze. "The founders of Granite hall."

The school was aptly named, T.J. thought.

"Mr. Hayward was kind enough to warn me you were coming."

"Warn you?"

"Notified me, would be a better way of putting it, I suppose. But you must understand that what happened to Joanne Kirkland all those years ago is painful to think or talk about."

"You were here when it happened?"

The woman smiled. It transformed her into something human. Her grey hair, cropped short, and her blue eyes framed by no-nonsense steel framed glasses no longer made her seem so grim. It was the starkness of the building, T.J. realized, that gave an erroneous first impression of its occupants.

"My dear, I've been here for more years than I care to think about. I was a student here myself. I left to pursue a career as a governess, came back here as a teacher, and was made head mistress many years ago. This place is my home, its pupils, the only family I have."

"Can you tell me about what happened here that might have caused Joanne to have a nervous breakdown?"

"Only what I know, and that is very little, I'm afraid. Joanne was found wandering around the grounds in the middle of the night." The older woman blushed. "She was quite naked, incoherent, and quite hysterical. I called a doctor, of course. Joanne was transferred to a hospital the next day. I never saw her again. Her parents had her flown back to America and to an institution there, so I understand."

"She was naked? Is it possible there was some form of sexual assault?"

Miss Bramfield pursed her lips. "Rumors flew like wild birds. Rape was one of the more ugly stories that were bandied about. Hawkins, our custodian at the time, received undue publicity, and undue blame. Joanne wasn't raped. Her parents assured me of that. They had her examined, and she was still a virgin. Nowadays, that's not too common a trait in young girls, is it?" She looked to T.J. for confirmation.

T.J. let the statement stand. "How did the rumors of rape get their start? What condition was she in, Miss Bramfield, when she was found?"

The older woman stood. She ran her fingers across her brow. "This is an all girl's school, Miss McCall. Idle gossip turned viscous. Too much was said involving Hawkins. Despite proof to the contrary, it was too late to salvage his reputation. He was branded from that night on. He left of his own accord rather than be dismissed. Not long after that he had a heart attack and died. Unrelated," She hastened to add, "to the incident here, of course." She shivered. "Every time I'm forced to think about that night I keep thinking that there was something I could have done. I'd almost managed to put the incident to rest. It happened so long, but then that young man came, and now you."

Every nerve ending was on edge when T.J. snapped, "What young man?"

"He said he was Joanne's husband. That he needed to know what happened that night so as he could help her with the nightmares.

"When was this?"

"Many years ago. Six or seven, I think. I'm sorry, but when you get to be my age time gets away from you."

"Could you identify this man from a photograph?"

"Yes...I mean I don't know. It was so long ago."

T.J. wished she had a picture of Michael Sinclair with her. She would have Pearl fax her one. "I'll bring a photograph of someone with me tomorrow."

"It wasn't her husband then?"

"Possibly. It could have been her first husband. From what I've heard about him it would be in character, only I don't think it was Joanne's welfare he was concerned with. Tell me everything you told him and anything else you might remember. Please. It's important. I don't want to hurt Joanne, I want to help her."

"It was a long time ago. As I've already mentioned, when we found Joanne she was stark naked."

"Abused?"

The woman gave her a hard look. "How could you know that?"

"A guess. How badly she was abused?"

The woman grimaced. "She was covered with blood. At first, it looked worse than it was. The blood came from many tiny puncture wounds on her chest, stomach, and thighs, none of them deep, all surface."

"Did she say anything? Anything at all in those first few minutes that you found her?"

Miss Bramfield sighed. "Only one clear word. Satan, that was it. She said it several times, and then she passed out." Miss Bramfield turned grey. T.J. thought she might be having a heart attack.

"Are you okay?"

"Yes." She sank back in the chair.

T.J. pressed on. "That look on your face. It was more than the horror of that night, wasn't it? You know what Joanne was alluding to?"

Resignation and regret filled Miss Bramfield's voice. "I never told anyone this before. No one ever asked. But, yes, I knew. There had been gossip about a hideous cult within the school, but there was always gossip. If you believed everything...I was going to do something about this particular gossip, but then Joanne...Joanne had the incident. If there was any strength to the rumor of a cult, we never proved it."

"Do you know the names of the girls involved?"

She shook her head. "No. Those that may have been involved protected each other. The others were too scared."

"Why, Joanne?"

"Maybe because she was the only American here at the time. Maybe it was all that money. I don't know. We've never had another incident like it. I swear it."

"I believe you. Do you remember the names of any of Joanne's friends?"

"That's an easy one. She never had any. Tell me, Miss McCall, what can you possibly gain by dragging this up all over again? How is this knowledge going to help you find Joanne's missing husband?"

T.J. placed her hand over Miss Bramfield's thin leathery fingers. "I don't know. I really don't know. But I think it's important. I just don't know why yet."

* * *

T.J. returned to the school the next day with a picture of Michael Sinclair. Miss Bramfield shook her head. "No. The man that came here was older. I remember now, he had a scar on his cheek, and he wore glasses. This man is too young, and much too good looking."

T.J. took the picture from her. "Thanks, anyway." She gave Miss Bramfield her card. "If you think of anything, anything at all, call me. You can reverse the charges."

T.J. left London the same day. She took one last look at England's shores as the plane began its long journey over the Atlantic Ocean. Too bad she hadn't really gotten to see anything. But, on the bright side, she felt that she had garnered some important information. Nothing she could use right away, but like all information, it would be stored away in her mind for future use.

* * *

She was home one full day when she received a call from Miss Bramfield. "Did you remember something else?" T.J. asked.

"No. Nothing more. But I thought you should know. The day you left, a man came. He said he worked for you, and that you'd forgotten to tape our conversation. He asked me if I'd repeat everything we talked about."

The hair on the back of T.J.'s neck stood up. "Did you?"

"I may be old, Miss McCall, and I may have been sheltered from life, but I'm not senile, nor am I foolish. I told him I'd have to check with you first. He said he'd be back, but he never returned."

"Thank you, Miss Bramfield, and I never meant to imply that your judgment couldn't be trusted. Can you describe him?"

T.J. listened while Miss Bradfield described the man. Her breathing quickened as she listened. The man that Miss Bramfield was describing could have been the man she'd met on that plane, right down to his too-blue eyes.

When the connection was severed, T.J. stared into space. If it was Mark Sanders who had gone to the school, his being on the same plane with her was no accident. He'd followed her to New York, then to London. But, why? Better yet, who or what was he? And what did he want?

Chapter Five

Gregg paid the cab driver and stared up at the palatial building and manicured grounds of Rosewood Retreat. He whistled. No wonder they didn't call it a sanitarium. It looked like a fucking castle!

The clipped tone on the other end of the phone when he'd called here yesterday informed him that Doctor Weatherly could spare him thirty minutes today. He would see Gregg at precisely 10:30 a.m.

It was 10:29.

Gregg passed though ten-foot high oak doors with beveled glass inserts that led into a thickly carpeted foyer. It didn't look even remotely like a hospital. It looked more like a high-class hotel. The receptionist didn't wear hospital whites, but then neither did any of the nursing staff. He wondered how much they charged here a day, and knew it had to be a bundle.

He was led down two corridors, also thickly carpeted, and into a large room lined with walnut bookcases. A mammoth oak and leather desk accommodated a leather swivel chair. Other furnishings included a leather couch, state-of-the-art stereo system, and a round glass-topped table with four chairs. In front of the huge desk were two leather arm chairs.

Doctor Weatherly was outfitted as expensively as the room. His Sax, Fifth Avenue suit cost more than most people made in a week. He was tall, almost bald, his nose aquiline, and his chin weak.

The doctor extended his hand and Gregg accepted it. It was cold and clammy. "Mr. Brooks. Please, take a seat wherever you feel comfortable."

"Thanks. Okay if I sit in your chair?" And at the doctor's frown, "It was a joke, Doc." Christ! He thought. People came to this room to get help? He took a seat on one of the chairs in front of the desk.

"You told my nurse that you wanted to talk to me about Joanne Kirkland. All I can tell you is that she was a model patient."

"If all I needed was sugar coating I'd have asked you to fax me a report. Listen, Doc, we can do this hard, or we can do it easy. You see, I didn't get to be one of the best investigators for a man of my tender years by accident. I've earned the title. Your patients aren't the only ones with skeletons in their closets."

It was a shot in the dark that sometimes worked. It worked now. "You're too modest. You left out the word ruthless. What is it you think I can tell you about Joanne that doesn't violate patient confidentiality?"

"I'll make it easy for you, Doc. No tough questions. You treated Joanne Kirkland yourself?"

"For the most part." He sighed. "Unfortunately, she wasn't one of my success stories."

"Really? Why was that?"

"She left here of sound mind, but then she wasn't crazy to begin with. We were just never able to get her to remember what happened to her in England, and we tried everything. And that's all I can tell, or will tell you."

Obviously Weatherly's skeletons weren't that scandalous. Gregg wondered if they resorted to shock therapy in this plush prison. A prison harsher than the real thing in so many ways because of the subterfuge, the gloss that concealed a sanitarium for the mentally unstable. He thought about the corridors he'd traveled to get here. There were no patients roaming the halls. Where did they keep them? "Everything?" he asked.

"Yes. You understand, of course, the only reason I agreed to see you, or even talk about Joanne, was because of the call I received from Charlton Hayward. But regardless of Mr. Hayward's high standing, I won't compromise either myself, or this place, by divulging our methods of treatment to a layman. Suffice to say, that we didn't, nor do we mistreat our guests here with such bizarre methods as shock therapy or by strapping them in their beds."

"You must have been reading my mind, Doctor. Will Joanne Kirkland ever remember what it was that sent her off the deep end?"

Weatherly shook his head. "Hard to say, but I doubt it."

Gregg stood. "Well, I guess that does it."

Weatherly frowned. He looked down at his watch. "We still have ten minutes."

Gregg leaned forward. "Use it one somebody who gives a shit, Doc. We both know you aren't going to tell me anything I can use. Putting the Hippocratic Oath aside, it's not your style. I'll see myself out."

* * *

On his way out of the building, Gregg gave the young blonde receptionist a big smile. He made note of the name rider. Tammy Underwood. She smiled back at him.

He made a note to himself to call her later.

* * *

The quest to interview Joanne's circle of friends was as futile as Gregg's visit to the sanitarium, and more frustrating. No one claimed any close personal ties to her. No one seemed to know what she felt, what she did with herself, or what she thought. But Gregg's efforts were not all in vain. Despite everyone's inability to supply information, none-the-less, a very clear picture of her was emerging. She was a loner.

It was time to connect with T.J.

* * *

T.J. stared at the photograph in her hand. The man was good-looking, blond, and blue-eyed. He had a great smile, and beautiful teeth. She looked up as Gregg entered her office and tucked the photograph in her top drawer. "You look tired, Gregg."

Gregg plopped down in a chair. "I am. Your girl is an enigma, T.J. A real loner. I don't know how she interacted with her husbands, but she sure as hell shut everyone else out."

"Except possibly Hayward, and he's not saying any more than he has to. I'm sure of it."

She came around the desk and perched herself on top. Gregg looked appreciatively at her legs.

"You want to run away with me, T.J.?" He said. "One night, anyway. Do you have any idea how many times I've fantasized about you and me under the same set of sheets?"

"No, and I don't want to know. Besides, you should be finding a girl your own age."

"You're not Grandma Moses. What do you have on me, eight, nine years?"

"It's the miles that count, Gregg. Now, can we get back to Joanne?"

He shrugged. "If we must. The sanitarium is run like a high-class hotel. I don't think any attempt is made to cure, just pamper until those who put them there decide to let them come home. All but a few of the clientele are victims of neurosis, though there were several inmates that qualify as certified loonies. I was able to find out that they are kept in a separate part of the building." He smiled to himself. Tammy Underwood had been accommodating in more ways that one. "If there was an attempt to help Joanne Kirkland, they're not talking about it."

"I got much the same reaction in London," T.J. said. "I guess it's time to follow David Sinclair's trail. If there is one," she added ruefully. She hesitated. "Something else, Gregg. About six or seven years ago a man was at the school asking questions about Joanne, and a man followed me to London. He said his name was Mark Sanders, but that was obviously an alias. He went to the boarding school after I did. He was checking up on me and what I may have found out."

"The same man who followed you was the guy who went to the boarding school before?"

"I don't think so."

Gregg whistled. "Then there is something to your theory that what happened to Joanne Kirkland all those years ago is relevant to her husband's disappearance. I have to admit, I thought you were barking up the wrong tree. Do you have a description of the guy that tailed you?"

T.J. eased herself off the desk. A frown etched lines in her face. "I was careless. I have this thing about flying. It seems to clog all the investigative skills I ever learned. He had dark curly hair, he wore a beard, and he had a moustache. My first impression was that he was in his thirties. Now, I'm not sure. His eyes were too blue. Contacts I think. All my instincts weren't neutralized, thank God. When he shook my hand I had the sense that something was wrong. Later, I realized what it was. The hairs on his hand were so blonde they were almost non-existent. It tracks that his hair is likely blond, and his eyes green, maybe blue, just not that blue."

"Not much to go one, T.J. But I'll check the airlines. Is it possible he followed you from here, or did you pick him up in New York?"

"I don't know."

Gregg stood. "What are you thinking, T.J.?"

"That it's possible I found David Sinclair. Or, he found me."

"What the hell makes you think it was David Sinclair on that plane?" Gregg exploded.

"A feeling. Nothing more."

"But why, for Christ's sake?"

"Now, there you have me, Gregg."

"And the guy who was at the boarding school six or seven years ago? You still don't think they were one and the same?"

T.J. frowned. "No...how could it be? Joanne and David were married only two years ago."

"Right. So what now, coach?"

"We talk to Joanne. She has to tell us more about David Sinclair. Something that will allow us to follow a trail as cold as Alaska in the dead of winter."

"And if the lady doesn't cooperate?"

"Then she can find herself another detective agency."

But as soon as the words left her lips, T.J. knew that the man on the plane, whoever the hell he was, had made this case so personal, that nothing was going to stop her from following the trail until there was no trail left to follow.

* * *

Joanne picked up the receiver. Her hands trembled. This time, like all the others in the past year, there was only music in the background, eerie, unmelodic music, and the sound of laughter. It was soft at first, and then it turned maniacal. And, like all the other times, she listened, unable to bear it, yet unable to keep from listening.

Only this time there was one big difference. When the laughter and the music stopped, a man's voice whispered. "I'm alive, Joanne. I'm alive."

"David!"

He laughed. It wasn't a pleasant sound. "You're such a romantic. How could I be David? David is dead, My Sweet."

"Then who…?"

"Don't you know?" More laughter.

Joanne cupped her hand over her mouth. "Oh, my God. Michael!"

But now there was only silence.

Chapter Six

It was an hour past sunset, yet Joanne made no attempt to turn on the light. She stared instead into the darkened void.

Michael.

It was easier to remember their beginnings. Back then she'd seen life through rose-colored glasses. In some ways it was a blessing to have been that naïve, even if the glow didn't last, because she had been blissfully happy for a while. She'd met Michael at art school. He was a very talented student, she little more than mediocre.

One evening, he made his way across the room to peek at her canvas. The model that night was a very handsome, much muscled, and a very nude Adonis.

There were only squiggly lines on her sketchpad. Michael laughed. "I've been watching you. You haven't once looked up at the model. Embarrassed?"

She blushed. Her inability to look at the naked model went beyond embarrassment. How, or even why, should she tell him that at the age of thirty-two she'd never had a man, nor even seen a man naked, not even her brother in his post-pubescent years. "It's not that, I'm just not very good at this." She blushed again. "But you are. I've taken a look at your work."

She was never sure just how he maneuvered her into accepting his invitation for coffee after class. All she knew was that she was terrified to be alone with him. In a matter of days he dispelled that fear, and she learned to relax around him. She began to tell him things about herself, describing the privileged environment in which she was raised, touching only briefly on her schooling in England. He, in turn, told her that he'd grown up in a succession of foster homes, his only kin a younger brother from whom he was mostly separated, and that he, too, had always felt lonely and different.

"But you're so handsome," she blurted out. "You could never be lonely except by design."

"And you?" he'd countered.

"I like being by myself."

"I don't believe you," he said. "Not for a minutes. I'm attracted to you, Joanne. Maybe it's your naiveté. It's so charming and so unexpected in a world where women come on to me at every turn. It's made me leery of women in general, but not of you. You're special." He took her hand in his. "Come to my place," he urged.

She pulled her hand away. "Why?"

His eyes locked with hers, refusing to let her look away. "I think you know why."

She'd given in to him. That night he opened the doors to pleasures she never dreamed existed. And that same night he asked her to marry him.

She remembered the look on Charlie's face when she introduced Michael as her husband, his look of disbelief. He'd taken her to one side. "You should have come to me first, Joanne. I always expected to investigate marital prospects before you took the oath."

"And you never once told me that Charlie, did you? You never did, because, like me, you never expected anyone to want me. I love him, Charlie. Don't spoil it for me."

Michael moved into the Kirkland mansion, and, for a while Joanne tiptoed through paradise never expecting it to end. But gradually Michael grew more and more remote. He seldom touched her any more. She was sure there were other women, and hadn't cared as long as he kept coming home to her, disgusted with herself for being weak and so dependent on him.

One night, unable to sleep as she stared at Michael's rigid back, wanting him but afraid to be rebuffed, and embarrassed to ask for his sexual favors, she made her way downstairs to get herself a glass of milk. As her feet touched the second step she felt something like a fist on her back, and then she was tumbling down the staircase.

When she came to, Michael was staring down at her, concern on his face. "Stay still, Joanne. We've called the doctor." He crushed her to him. "My God, I almost lost you tonight."

He cared! It was all she could think about. Michael cared!

The next day, Charlie brought her back to reality. "I don't think it was an accident, Joanne. I think Michael tried to harm you, possibly kill you."

"I don't believe you!"

"It's true. I can't prove it, but I feel it here." He jabbed his fist into his stomach. "If you'd only admit it, so do you. But you don't have to worry about him anymore. I told Michael that your death will win him nothing financially. I think you're safe now. He won't try to hurt you again."

She'd rather have been dead. She was safe, so Charlie said. And never more alone. Michael was truly lost to her now.

After his talk with Charlie, Michael made no pretense of his contempt for Joanne. He moved into a guest room, and now he didn't even try to hide his numerous affairs.

She was getting ready to file for divorce the morning Michael left for the lake. It was the last time she'd seen him.

* * *

The road to Joanne's home was on a curved stretch of road. T.J. checked her watch. 10:12 p.m. Joanne had sounded agitated when she'd called. It must be important to want to bring T.J. out this late.

There was a glimmer of a tail light in the far distance only visible when T.J. drove on an infrequent straight stretch of road. It was the first and only car she'd seen in the last five minutes. Few people lived this far out of town. She shivered. Come one, she cautioned herself. It's just a car. Don't make something out of it.

When T.J.'s car entered the driveway of Joanne's home, the front door of the house sprang open. Joanne ushered her inside.

"Sorry to call you this late," Joanne said. "I feel so foolish now. Would you like some coffee?"

"A glass of wine would be better. Coffee keeps me awake. And don't feel bad about calling me. I wanted to talk to you anyway, but I was going to wait until morning. But now that I'm here..."

"I'll get the wine."

When Joanne came back she had two full glasses in her hand. Wine for T.J., a screwdriver for herself. "How was your trip to London?"

"Interesting. But let's get to what prompted you to call me this late at night." She shot forward in her chair. "My God, Joanne, your hands are shaking. You're frightened. What's happened?"

Joanne jerked to her feet. "It's the phone calls. I've been getting them for months. Until tonight all they consisted of were weird music and laughter. Maniacal, unbalanced laughter." Joanne shivered and took a large gulp of her drink.

"And, tonight?" T.J. prompted.

"He spoke. It was the first time. I thought it was David. They sounded so much alike."

T.J. involuntarily shuddered. "Who sounded so much alike?"

"David and Michael. But it wasn't David. He said he was dead. It was Michael, and he said that David was dead."

"Your first husband called here!"

"Yes. They never found his body, you know, but I believed he was dead." She wrung her hands together. "If he isn't dead why didn't he come forward before?"

"It could have been a prank call. Are you so sure it was Michael?"

Joanne stared back at her, a look of hope on her face. "Prank call? Do you think so?"

"It's possible, but it's more important for me to know what you believe."

The look of hope disappeared. Joanne shook her head vehemently. "It was Michael."

"All right, let's assume for a minute it was. Why call you after all these years?"

"Perhaps, because he killed David."

"But they're brothers!"

"But not close. Not even friends, really."

T.J. looked thoughtful. "Tell me how and when you met David," she said.

Joanne swallowed. T.J. had the distinct impression that she had forgotten T.J. was in the room. Joanne was off in another dimension, in another time and place. A much happier time and place.

* * *

Joanne and Michael had been married for over a year, Joanne told T.J., when David appeared in her life for the first time. By then her marriage was only a sham.

He'd materialized one day without warning. Michael was off someplace, God knows where. Probably with another of his endless floozies.

It was the housekeeper's day off. He appeared suddenly on the threshold of the solarium where Joanne was tending an ailing violet, his slim body bathed in sunlight, like a vision. She looked up, squinted, and pushed a stray hair out of her eyes, brushing her hand across her cheek, leaving a smudge of dirt.

He extended his hand. He and Michael were about the same height, over six-feet, blond and blue-eyed, both engagingly handsome. There the similarity ended. Where Michael was self-assured, aggressive, David was soft-spoken, retiring. His eyes expressed a sensitivity she'd never seen in Michael's.

"Sorry to barge in like this," he said. "It's not like Michael and I are close." He grinned. "Fact is, he'll probably be glad he missed me."

Joanne removed her utility gloves. "Then, why come?"

"You're direct. I like that. I was curious about the woman Michael married. I read up on you and your family, and your marrying my brother didn't make much sense. Meeting you now, I'm more puzzled."

Joanne flushed. "Why? Because I'm not beautiful?"

"Oh, my God, no! I mean...I didn't mean...Damn. What a lousy beginning this is."

"And an appropriate ending. Your brother married me for my money. You can leave now with your curiosity satisfied." She turned her back on him.

"I'm so sorry. I've hurt you. I didn't mean to. It was Michael's motives I was questioning. He's a louse. How could he have attracted someone as genteel as you? And you underestimate yourself. Beauty comes in more than one dimension."

She whirled around. "For a moment it sounded like you meant that!"

"I did. Tell Michael I'm sorry I missed him." He grinned. "On second thought, don't tell him that. He'd know I was lying. Can we be friends, do you think?"

She wanted him to stay. He was everything she'd thought and hoped Michael would be. But she had no right. "There's no room in my life for friends. But if you'd like, I won't tell Michael that you were here."

"Thanks. At least that's a friendly gesture. Maybe we'll see each other again."

She wanted that more than anything. She knew it was up to her to decide whether she wanted him in her life. She could let it happen, make it happen. She looked wistful. She wasn't ready. "I doubt it. But before you go tell me why you and Michael are so distant. I had a brother who died young. We weren't close either, but I loved him. I sense that you don't even like Michael."

"You're very intuitive." He took her hand and kissed it. "I'm so glad we met."

She hadn't told Michael about his visit. The next time David appeared in her life was at the memorial service she'd held for Michael a week after he drowned.

Except now it looked like Michael hadn't drowned after all.

* * *

It rained the day of the memorial service. There were few mourners. Joanne, Charlton, the servants, and, and she was still horrified by the memory of it, members of the press who easily outnumbered them.

She hadn't been aware that David was there until the service was over. He was there at her elbow, shielding her from rabid reporters before she realized what he was doing.

He drove back to the house with her, quietly taking charge in such a gentle unassuming manner that even Charlie seemed willing to go along with Joanne, allowing David to assume the role of protector.

He stayed in the guest cottage that adjoined the Kirkland estate for over a month, joining her for meals after she dismissed the servants.

The first time she felt his kiss, she knew that she loved him and that she had loved him from that first moment a year ago. As amazing as it seemed to her, he loved her, too. Really loved her, not like Michael who had only pretended to care.

They talked about Michael sporadically. He, with a sadness, born she suspected, from their lack of closeness, and she, more often than not, with bitterness. She found she could remember nothing good about her relationship with Michael, only the pain.

Eventually, she moved David into a nearby apartment building sneaking out of the Kirkland mansion at night to be with him.

After their marriage Joanne arranged for them to stay in a motel until the current house was completed. On their wedding night he made love to her five times. She was surprised at his passion, and even more with her own, and then consumed by it.

Then he'd disappeared, just like Michael. But unlike Michael, he'd left a hole in her heart that would never heal.

* * *

T.J. listened as Joanne relived the past. She experienced a moment of envy. She'd loved Jim with the fierceness of a lioness, loved Scott now with all her heart, but she'd never felt anything remotely resembling the almost fantasy-like passion of the woman who sat across from her. She put out her hand. "If he's alive, Joanne, I'll find him." She'd started to say and bring him back to you, but the mental image of the man on the plane stopped her. If it was David who'd followed her to London, it was not the David of Joanne's memories.

"He's dead, T.J., Michael said so."

"If it was Michael on the phone, how could he know that?"

"Because he killed him."

T.J. felt a chill run down her spine. "You can't really believe that!"

"I have to. Because if Michael didn't kill David, then maybe I did."

And with that, her eyes glazed over.

Shaken, T.J. passed her hand in front of Joanne's eyes, but they didn't flicker. Joanne had slipped into a trance-like state.

Chapter Seven

Despite T.J.'s efforts to coax Joanne back to normal, and her insistence that she explain the declaration that she might have killed David, Joanne remained mute, almost catatonic. T.J. remembered Pearl telling her that a doctor who practiced in town, lived out here somewhere. His name was Graham or something like that. She flipped through the phone book, constantly looking over at Joanne for signs of recovery. When she found the entry she wanted, a Doctor Roger Grathers, she dialed the number and waited for the service to put her through.

Doctor James Grathers was a no-nonsense individual in his fifties, who lived a few miles down the road in one of the few houses that dotted the landscape between here and town. He made no bones about his curiosity concerning the owner of the house.

"I watched this house being built off and on. I wondered about its inhabitants. There's so few of us out here I'd hoped to get to know them."

"You never met Joanne before tonight then, or her husband?"

"Never. Now, what happened here?"

It was too complicated to go into, even if T.J. wanted to, which she didn't. "She went into this state that you see. It was sudden. One moment she was talking to me, the next she was like this."

"You're a friend?"

"Not exactly. I work for Mrs. Sinclair."

Doctor Grathers looked over at Joanne. "It looks like a psychological condition, which is not my field. I don't know that I can help her. I can recommend someone."

"Isn't there something you can do? My boyfriend is a psychologist. I can talk to him tomorrow, or I can have her taken to a hospital now."

"Who is he?"

T.J. and the doctor swiveled around.

"Joanne?" T.J. said. "You were…you were ill. I called a doctor. This is your neighbor, Doctor Grathers."

"Don't be silly, I'm fine."

"At least let him check you out."

Joanne was agitated. "All right, but I'm not happy with you, T.J. I'm tired. I think I'll go to bed."

Doctor Grathers followed Joanne to her room. He emerged ten minutes later. "She seems to be all right now," he said. "She refused medication, but she was almost asleep when I left her."

"I'll go in and say goodnight, then."

He stopped her. "She said for you to leave. She wants to be left alone. I think its best. If I were you, I'd let your friend see her."

"Of course."

"Just what exactly do you do for Mrs. Sinclair?"

"I'm a private investigator. Joanne's husband is missing. She hired me to find him."

"And you came here with bad news?"

"Now listen here, Doctor Grathers, for the record I had nothing to do with Joanne's condition. She brought it on herself. But if she doesn't need me…" she looked down at her watch. "It's late, and if there's nothing I can do, I'd like to leave. You're sure she'll be all right?"

"I'd say so. I hate to press a point, but what is wrong with her?"

T.J. stared past him. "You're the doctor."

"That isn't what I mean, as well you know it."

T.J. sighed. "I didn't mean to be flip. Joanne will know no peace of mind, and neither will I, until I find out what happened to her husband. It's been a long day, Doctor. I really would like to go home."

They left the house together. It was almost 1:00 a.m. when T.J. pulled out of the driveway. For a while she followed the doctor's tail lights until he pulled off into a driveway of a house that sat way back from the road.

The winding country road was dark, deserted, no moon overhead. Then suddenly, she was no longer alone on the highway. The headlights of another car, its bright lights blinding her from behind, appeared from out of nowhere. Annoyed, T.J. slowed down so the car could pass, but it made no attempt to do so.

T.J. cursed under her breath. She waved the car on. Still, the vehicle made no attempt to pass.

"To hell with this," T.J. muttered. She pulled off to the side of the road.

The car sped by.

T.J. waited a few minutes then pulled out onto the open road. She was beginning to feel more at ease, ashamed of her earlier apprehension, when a few miles down the road, strong headlights once again hit her mirror, assaulting the interior of her car.

"Damn! He must be drunk," T.J. uttered aloud. She accelerated in an attempt to put distance between herself and the car behind her, and for a while the maneuver worked. The headlights of the other car disappeared.

It was at the curviest part of the road that the car appeared again, far too close for comfort. She slowed, and for a moment it looked as if the car would pass, and then it was alongside her, and with brutal impact the vehicle rammed itself into the driver's side of her car.

T.J. struggled with the steering wheel. This guy was worse than drunk, he was a maniac!

The car rammed her again, then again. Adrenalin pushed through her as the shock of impact after impact, and the insanity of the action itself, took its toll. She clutched the steering wheel tightly in an effort to hug the right-hand side of the road, overreacted, and steered too far to the right. The passenger side of her car hit a boulder, shuddered, and her world turned upside down as the car tumbled into a ditch wrong side up, hurtling her up against the passenger door.

Something warm and sticky trickled into her glazed green eyes. Stunned, but still conscious, she gingerly felt the top of her head, wet from her own blood. She tried to move, and was almost rendered unconscious by a piercing stab of pain in her side. She fought for control and willed herself not to pass out. She took a careful breath. Her nostrils were assailed with the odor of gas fumes.

She tried to swallow, but her mouth was dry, scratchy. Her breath came in short quick gaps. Her mother had died in a fiery plane crash. It was the memory of her mother's instant cremation that drove T.J. to action. She tried to push on the driver's door with her foot but the pain was too intense. She looked for another means of escape, eyeing the window. T.J. slowly turned and worked the handle, muttering, "Thank God for older cars." Every movement causing her to cry out, and the effort bringing tears to her eyes. She gritted her teeth, and finally the hole was large enough to crawl through. She instinctively reached for her cell phone, and carefully edged her way out. T.J. fell into the dirt floor below, clutching at her ribs, and crept one terrifying inch at a time, stopping only to wipe blood from her eyes, clinging to the phone she viewed as her lifeline.

She was barely out of harms way when her car exploded and became a raging inferno. T.J. cringed. A few more seconds and she would have been burned alive.

She peered at the road beyond. A roar filled her head that she mistook for warning of a pending blackout, until she realized it was the sound of a car idling in the darkness, its lights out. The sound was suppressed as her own car boomed into a ball of fire once again. It was a sound she would never forget. The other car, satisfied no doubt that she couldn't have survived the explosion, sped off into the distance.

T.J. began to shake. It was no longer a question of a drunk or careless driver. Whoever was in that car had deliberately run her off the road. Someone thought she was closer to a solution to this case than she was.

Intense pain rocked her body. She was alone out here with no one within earshot. She could scream all night and no one would hear her.

The phone! Had it survived the impact of the crash, its workings intact and unimpaired? She slowly and painfully dialed 911, a silent prayer on her lips.

Chapter Eight

Marshall showed up while she was still in the emergency room. When they'd wheeled T.J. in and asked who she wanted to call, his was the first name to leave her lips. Calling Scott could wait.

She'd been lucky, the intern said. Aside from bruises and cuts, all she'd suffered was a mild concussion and two cracked ribs. She also had her life.

"What happened, T.J.?" Marsh asked. "If it was just an accident you wouldn't have called me."

She tried to raise her head from the gurney. The room began to spin and the doctor in attendance chastised her for her attempt. "Good instinct, Marsh," T.J. said. "That's what I like about you, among other things. Someone ran me off the road after I left Joanne's house."

He shook his index finger at her. "You gave me quite a scare. When they called and said you'd had an accident..." he shook his head. "I buried your father because he was reckless, I don't want to bury you for the same reason. Didn't I warn you about fooling around with that broad?" He edged closer to her. "Want to fill me in?"

She attempted a smile. "Don't worry, Marsh, I'm not looking to die. And I'll tell you as much as I can." She told him about her trip to London, but not the reason why she'd gone there. She told him about the man on the plane and about the calls Joanne had been getting.

He sighed. "You know that I know who Joanne is, T.J. I know all about her first husband, and I know about the incident in

England, and her being locked up in a nut house. So quit playing cute, and tell me all you know."

T.J. couldn't do that, but she could tell him parts of it. "Joanne thinks the calls are from her first husband, Michael. He was David's brother, but you probably know that, too." A shooting pain impacted her side with the force of a knife. She grimaced.

Concern lined his face. "Maybe this should wait."

"No, I'm okay." And at his look of disbelief. "Really, Marsh."

"All right. But if you pass out on me, there'll be hell to pay from the doctors."

"I'm okay. Go on."

"Stubborn, just like your old man. He'd have been proud of you, T.J."

She felt tears sting her eyes. She missed her father.

"You're right," Marsh went on pretending not to notice her tears. "I know about the bastard's phone call, Got it from Pearl. Under protest, of course."

"Ah, yes. The third degree Pearl told me about. The man who called Joanne told her that David was dead." T.J. stared steadfastly at Marsh. She couldn't tell him that Joanne, subject to blackouts, was afraid she'd killed David herself. Client confidentiality aside, T.J. didn't believe that Joanne was capable of murder, and certainly not of killing a man she'd loved that much.

"You're hiding something, T.J. What the hell did you stumble into that someone wanted to kill you to keep it quiet?"

She frowned. "That's the scary part, Marsh. Nothing I can think of. All I have are pieces of a puzzle that won't come together. Fragments. Did you come up with anything?"

"Dead ends. But you worried the hell out of someone, that's for sure. Did you get a make on the car or a description of the driver?"

"Not really. The car was dark, a sedan I think. Maybe a Ford or a small Lincoln. Or it could have been a Cadillac. Hell, Marsh, it could have been anything. I was too busy trying to stay on the road. I only caught a glimpse of the driver. He wore a coat pulled up around his neck and a hat."

"You're a big help."

"Sorry."

"Did you call Scott?"

"Yes. He'll be here soon. And, Marsh? I told him it was an accident. That I missed a turn in the road. You're the only one that knows this was more than an accident."

"Is that wise?"

"You know how Scott worries, and how he hates my work. Please don't tell him."

Marsh hesitated. "Okay, T.J. But I'll have a patrol car check up on you round the clock."

"No! Scott isn't stupid. He'd know, or suspect I was in danger." She shrugged, and then winced. "Damn, that hurt. Thanks, Marsh. Besides, whoever it was probably won't be foolish enough to try again."

Marsh looked worried. "I wouldn't be so goddamn sure."

*　*　*

Scott arrived shortly after Marsh left while T.J. was being transferred into a room. T.J., though sore and lightheaded, was irritated at being confined to a hospital bed for two days.

"What the hell, T.J.!" Scott blurted out.

"I'm fine. Thanks for asking!" She countered his anger.

He took her hand. "Sorry. I almost had my own accident rushing over here. Are you okay?"

"Nothing a tube of Bengay and a vial of Tylenol won't cure. Seriously, I'm fine."

"How'd it happen?"

She'd been rehearsing her response to his question from the moment she'd told him it was an accident. She hated to lie to him. "I was tired. Joanne said some startling things. I was thinking, instead of watching the road."

"You could have been killed."

She shivered. "I know."

He frowned. "I want you off this case, T.J."

"No! We've never interfered with each other's professional lives, Scott. Let's not start now. Anyway, I was going to ask you to help me with Joanne."

"How? And I'm not saying I will." He hastily added.

She smiled. The gesture hurt. She raised up the hospital bed. "Joanne suffers from blackouts. She has for years. Nothing serious, so she says. But now she thinks she may have done something terrible during one of them." She paused. "Like killing her husband."

"That's a bizarre and gruesome twist. What do you want me to do?"

"Talk to her. They let me call her from the emergency room. She's agreed to see you. I want to know, and so does she, if she's capable of violence."

He tilted her chin with her fingertips. "And you don't think she is."

"No. But I'm not the expert."

He moved away from the bed to the window. "If I say yes, will you agree to drop the case if, given the right circumstances, I detect an inclination for violence in Joanne?"

"And, if I say, no?"

"Damn, you're a stubborn woman. Maybe that's why I love you so much. Okay, I'll see Joanne. When are they going to let you out of here?"

"Tomorrow, the day after, I don't know. Gregg is going to take over for me."

"Good. Maybe he'll have this case whipped by the time they turn you loose."

But neither he nor T.J. really believed that.

* * *

Marshall responded to a tap on his shoulder. He frowned. "T.J.! Should you be out of the hospital? And how the hell did you get here? You didn't drive, did you?"

"Yes to your first question, and no I didn't drive here. I took a cab. Satisfied?"

"Not really. What can I do for you? Say you've decided to let us handle the Joanne Sinclair, Kirkland thing and you'll make me a very happy cop. Gut instinct tells me that if you don't, we'll end up butting heads. I wouldn't like that."

"Neither would I. I came to ask a favor."

"Is granting it going to get my ass in a sling?"

She grinned. "I don't think so. I told you about the man on the plane. I have to know who he is. Can I use your police artist?"

"Who do you think it was?"

"Damn it, Marsh, you know I can't tell you that. Not yet. But I will. I promise."

He sighed. "Okay. But, it's the last favor from me you get on this goddamn thing until you tell me all you know. And I mean everything."

He dialed an extension. "Paul, T.J. McCall is coming over. She wants a composite. Give it to her...this time." He hung up. A frown crossed his face. "Did a patrol car follow you over here?"

She bent over and kissed him. "Just like you ordered." She sobered. "I want them off me, Marsh. Not only because of Scott, but because I can't function with a black and white up my butt. Promise?"

"Stubborn, just like your old man," he muttered. "All right, as of now they're off you."

"You wouldn't lie to me," she said good naturedly.

"Only if I thought I had a chance of getting away with it. Now, get the hell out of here. I have work to do."

* * *

Paul Kaplan was an elfish little man with magic in his pencil. Thirty minutes after T.J. described the man on the plane, an almost perfect likeness stared back at her from his sketchpad.

"Perfect," she said. "Now, can you make him a little older, then younger, take away the beard and make his hair lighter. The nose, too, may have been puffed out. Give him a longer more sculptured nose."

Fifteen minutes later she was looking at the composite. It could have been either of the Sinclair brothers since they looked so much alike.

* * *

T.J. stopped by Scott's downtown office. His appointment with Joanne had been scheduled for this morning at her home. Impatient to know the outcome, T.J. didn't want to wait until tonight to talk to him about the session.

She waited in the outer office until he was between appointments. His receptionist announced her.

Scott embraced her, and then gently pushed her away. "Why didn't you let me pick you up from the hospital?"

"I was anxious to get away from there."

"And you're okay?"

"Fine. How'd it go with Joanne?"

Scott eased her into a chair. "It didn't. She let me in, then nicely, but firmly, told me that she'd changed her mind about talking to me."

"You let her get away with that!"

"I can't make her talk to me, T.J."

"Great! Maybe I should run out there and talk to her."

"Forget it."

T.J. sighed. "You're right, of course. How did she seem to you?"

"In better shape than you are. Why don't you go home and rest?"

T.J. was suddenly overwhelmingly tired. "Maybe I will. Will you be home early?"

He kissed her. "As soon as I can get away. Missed me in your bed have you?"

"What kind of question is that to ask a lady? But, yes, I missed you like hell. God, how I've missed you."

Scott gave her a long hard stare. "For a moment you sounded almost...almost...I don't know. Are you sure you're all right?"

She wanted to fold herself into the warmth of his arms. She wanted to be held. She wanted to tell him that someone had tried to kill her. She wanted to tell him that she was scared, and not just because of the attempt on her life, but because she felt vulnerable and somehow alone. She did none of it. "I'm just tired. Hurry home."

* * *

Despite Scott's urging to take one more day to rest, T.J. went into the office the next day. She whizzed past Pearl. "Get Gregg over here, Pearl."

"Yes Ma'am. Are you sure you should be out and around? You look like hell."

"Thanks. You're beautiful, too, Pearl."

Pearl followed T.J. into her office. T.J. flipped though the stack of mail on the desk. "Please. I know you mean well, don't coddle me. I had a minor accident, a few bruises and a couple of cracked ribs. I didn't die, and I'm not crippled. Save your concern for someone who needs it."

"I know that tone, T.J. It's a front for something you don't want me to know."

"Between you and Scott I'm liable to get a complex." She tried staring Pearl down. It didn't work."

"Then it wasn't an accident."

"I didn't say that."

"You didn't have to. Not to me anyway. I'll bring you some coffee, and then I'll try to find Gregg." Concern and frustration fused deep lines on her face.

T.J. ignored the remark and the look of distress. "Thanks."

Gregg arrived forty-five minutes later. He plopped himself down in a chair by T.J.'s desk. "You look terrible."

"So I keep hearing. What have you managed to find out?"

"Not much, and that bothers the hell out of me. David Sinclair just vanished. No one around here ever saw him. There's no credit card trail. Nothing. I checked into his background. I thought I might find something there."

"Did you?"

"All he had was the brother who supposedly drowned. Their father left when the boys were small, mother died of cancer shortly after. They were shunted back and forth to foster homes, separated most of the time. As they grew older they drifted apart. They didn't see each other for years after David ran away from his last foster home at the age of sixteen. Then, only briefly."

"Good work." Silently, T.J. conceded there was good reason for the two brothers to drift apart. They'd had less than ideal childhoods.

"What about the years before David married Joanne?"

Gregg shrugged. "Drew pretty much of a blank on that, too. David was a recluse. Probably a side effect of a troubled childhood. Not even the servants saw him. This is really interesting. Joanne really went to great lengths to live a secret existence. There's no official record of a marriage to David Sinclair. Looks like your little Miss-Goodie-Two-Shoes was living in what my grandmother used to call 'sin'. Don't you think it's time you started to seriously consider the possibility that David Sinclair is dead, T.J.?"

"I never ruled that out." She told him about her conversations with Joanne.

He whistled. "If I was Marsh I'd call out the dogs, literally. And I'd be looking for a body at Joanne's place."

"And if David isn't dead?"

"You don't believe that."

She showed him the composite that Paul had made for her. "The man on the plane could have been David or Michael."

"Or someone else."

"Like who?"

"Unlikely, I know. I don't think that Michael Sinclair is dead. I think it was most likely him who you met on the plane to London."

T.J. nodded. It made sense. "What do you suggest I do?"

"Give everything you know to Marsh. Let him handle it." Gregg eased himself out of the chair. "Did I tell you that you look like death warmed over?"

"You, and everyone else. I'll think about letting Marsh take over."

"Really? For how long will you think about it?"

She made a playful whack at him. "Damn it, I hate being predictable.

* * *

T.J. had been on the phone all day. Surely no one could disappear as effectively as had David Sinclair. And yet it seemed like both the Sinclair brothers had a knack for accomplishing that feat. On a hunch, she had Pearl check with Interpol for information on either Michael or David. Her last call of the day was to Charlton Hayward.

"I have reason to believe that Michael Sinclair is alive," she said.

"Nonsense. I admit I harbored no affection or even a small liking for the man, but in his defense I ask you the question why he would want to fake his own death? What could he hope to gain?"

"I haven't figured that one out yet. You told me what happened to the Kirkland fortune if Joanne dies, Counselor, but what happens to it if she is declared incompetent?"

"I wondered when you'd get around to asking that question. Joanne's parents' will leaves me in charge of managing the estate until, or if, Joanne recovered from any mental incapacity."

"I see."

"You only think you do, Miss McCall. I would challenge anyone who sought to declare Joanne incompetent. "And," anger crept into his voice, "though I understand the need to ask the question, I strongly resent the implication that I am in involved in any way with what is happening to Joanne now."

T.J. smiled. "Funny, Counselor, I don't recall implying anything. But it's something to ponder." She hung up before he could react. "Chew on that for a while," she muttered.

* * *

It was after midnight. Scott was sound asleep, but T.J. was restless. She rolled over in the bed. A strong acrid odor assailed her nostrils. Smoke!

She slipped out of the bed. She placed slippers on her feet and made her way down the hallway. The smell of smoldering ashes became stronger.

She ran back into the bedroom. She shook Scott. "Wake up. The house is on fire."

He jolted upright. He slipped on a robe and took her by the hand. Together they made their way down the hall. T.J. gasped. At the end of the hallway that led into the living room, there was a wall of smoke threatening to turn into flames. A small fire erupted and spilled into the hall, threatening to trap them.

T.J. was mesmerized. Her mother had died in a blanket of fire. Now, a fiery death was reaching out to claim her, too. Not once, but twice. First the car, now the house.

"Window," Scott gasped, covering his mouth with the collar of his robe, pulling her backwards into the bedroom, closing the door behind him. He yanked on the window. It was stuck. "It won't open. Stand back." He reached for a lamp and shoved it through the window. The sound of glass shattered the night air, and in the distance the sound of a siren.

Scott tried to guide her through the gaping hole that had once been a pane of glass. "My photo albums," she cried out. "They're all I have left of my parents. I have to go back inside and get them."

"I'll do it. And you're wasting time. We have to get out of here." He inhaled smoke and coughed. "Now, come on. Do as I say."

He pushed her outside, careful to keep her away from the jagged edges of glass. She fell to the grass below.

T.J. waited for him to follow. She could see flames fanning under the door of the bedroom, but she could no longer see Scott through the dense smoke.

"Scott, where are you?" She screamed.

She was still screaming as a fiery explosion blew the bedroom door off its hinges.

Chapter Nine

The wail of the ambulance siren filled the early morning air. It echoed like a scream in T.J.'s head, like the sound that came from the bedroom, Scott's cry of pain as the fire reached out to claim him, and like the scream she hadn't been able to stop at the scene of the fire until a kindly, but firm firefighter had slapped her. He'd taken her aside and calmed her, while the other firefighters doused the fireball that had once been her home.

She hadn't had to call Marsh; he was waiting for her when the ambulance carrying Scott arrived at the hospital. He held her back as hospital personnel took charge and wheeled Scott away. He was gentle, yet determined. "They don't need you in the way, T.J. Let them do their job."

She trembled uncontrollably. "It's my fault, Marsh. He stayed behind to get my photo albums." She choked. "Dear God, I didn't know the fire was that much out of control. One minute it was just smoke, and then it was a wall of fire." She bit down on her lip and drew blood. "I shouldn't have mentioned the damned albums. Now Scott is..." she clung to Marshall, her body wracked with sobs. "They won't tell me anything, Marsh. Can you find out how badly he's hurt?"

"I'll try. You want some coffee?"

She shook her head. "No. I just want Scott to be all right. I want to start last night all over again and change things."

Marshall held her in his arms. "I know, T.J. I know."

He returned fifteen minutes later. He had a plastic tumbler of water in one hand, a pill in the other. "The doctor said to take this. You've been through a lot."

"What is it?"

"A tranquilizer."

"No!"

"For God's sake, T.J., take it. If you won't do it for yourself, then do it for me."

The grim look on his face warned her that the news wasn't good. But then she'd known that from the time the firefighters had carried Scott outside. He was burned over more than three-quarters of his body. At least his face had been spared. "What did they say?"

"I won't try to con you, T.J. I didn't do that the night your father died, and I won't start now. It's bad. They're getting ready to move Scott to a burn center."

"I want to go with him."

"Spare him that, T.J. He's conscious now, and in a lot of pain. He wouldn't want you to see him this way."

"I've already seen what the fire did to him." She shivered. "But you're probably right. Will he make it, Marsh?"

He shrugged. "I don't know." What he didn't say was that it would be better if Scott didn't survive his horrendous injuries.

* * *

At Marsh's insistence T.J. allowed him to take her home with him. Gillian Holling, Marsh's wife, was waiting up for them. She settled T.J. in the spare bedroom, but T.J. couldn't sleep. Every time she closed her eyes she saw the bedroom door flying off its hinges, and she heard Scott crying out.

She dragged herself into the kitchen and poured herself a glass of cooking sherry that she found in a cupboard.

Marshall joined her in a few minutes later. "I couldn't sleep either. Want to talk about it?"

How very much she cared for this tough yet gentle man. "I can't. Not until I know if Schott is going to pull through."

"Then let's talk about the fire itself. I called the fire marshal. They'll sift through the ashes in the morning, but right now they don't think it was a natural fire.

"Arson!"

"Looks like. We'll know more in the morning."

T.J. forgot the glass and lifted the bottle of sherry to her lips. "Call Pearl in the morning and tell her to turn everything on the Sinclair case over to you."

"Considering that's what I want to hear, you'll change your mind, knowing you. You're upset, now. We'll discuss it in the morning."

"No. I've made my decision."

"And you're sure that's what you want?"

"Very sure. I'm only sorry I didn't do it sooner. If I had, Scott might not be fighting for his life now."

* * *

Pearl shook her head and clucked when T.J. entered the office. "What are you doing here? I sent all the information on the Sinclair case over to Marshall, and we have no other cases right now. Why don't you go on home?"

"Home? I don't have a home anymore."

"I'm sorry, I meant you shouldn't be here. You need to rest."

"It's okay, Pearl, you don't have to walk on eggshells. I've got myself a room in a hotel until...until I hear something. I went back to the house, or what's left of it. I see Scott everywhere, even in the rubble." She shivered. "I could even smell his after shave. Silly, isn't it?" She drew back her shoulders. "So, you see, I have to stay busy or I'll go crazy. I wanted to drive up to the Burn Center, but they told me Scott is unconscious again." A tear trickled down her cheek. "A blessing, I suppose, considering how badly he's burned."

T.J.'s tone was dangerously matter of fact, despite the moisture in her eyes. It was a defense, Pearl knew, for the hysteria she was holding at bay. "Then let's close the office, and I'll take you home with me."

"And do what? Thanks Pearl, but I'll be all right. Did you get anything from Interpol?"

"I thought you were off the case."

"I am. I'm just curious."

"I got some information, but like I said, I sent everything over to Marshall."

"But you do remember what you got from Interpol?"

"Not all of it," Pearl hedged.

T.J.'s eyebrows came together in a frown. "I was just making conversation, Pearl, but now you've got my interest. Just what did you learn from Interpol?"

Pearl sighed. "Oh, what the hell. As usual your instincts were good. David Sinclair ran away from his last foster home when he was sixteen. Nothing much is known about him until three years later when he hit Interpol's list as an enterprising nineteen-year-old master thief, and soldier of fortune. He must have gotten some education in those three years. Then, the CIA got in the act."

T.J. knew her mouth must be open. David Sinclair a villain! It didn't track with the picture Joanne had given of him. "Why, the CIA?"

"Because, after David graduated from stealing jewels and artwork, he started to steal secrets."

"For whom?"

"Now, there you have me. But it wasn't our side he stole for, I can tell you that. And I can only squeeze so much out of a computer before I hit a blank wall."

"And, Michael Sinclair?"

"He was employed by the CIA to locate his brother with the lure of amnesty for David Sinclair if he could bring him back."

T.J. shook her head in wonder. It was amazing the information Pearl could glean from a computer and her other sources. But Michael Sinclair in the role of knight in shining armor was another strange parallel. From all T.J. had heard about Michael Sinclair, he'd hardly seemed the type to put anything on the line for anyone, not even his own brother.

"Is there evidence that Michael Sinclair found David?"

"Briefly. Then they lost touch. Maybe David Sinclair sensed a trap. You can't live on the edge for long without building up some kind of inner radar."

"A trap?"

Pearl sniffed. "You can be sure there was one. I never did trust the government."

T.J. grinned in spite of the seriousness of the information Pearl was imparting. Pearl, before she'd come to work for T.J., had worked for the IRS fraud squad. She was not only able to use the bureaucracy she had so little regard for; she knew all of its inherent quirks and failings. "What's the latest on David Sinclair?"

"He disappeared without a trace ten years ago.'

T.J. looked thoughtful. "And he's still doing it. But it does explain why he was so guarded, and why he didn't want anyone to see him, he was afraid he might be recognized. It also explains his changing his name. I wonder how he justified his paranoia about being around people to Joanne."

"Marshall can ask her that," Pearl said pointedly.

"Right," T.J. murmured. But Pearl was not comforted.

The shrill ring of the phone on Pearl's desk forestalled further probing. She handed the phone to T.J. "It's for you. It's the Burn Center." She looked concerned.

T.J. took the receiver from her. She listened. Pearl felt a shiver run down her spine as she watched T.J.'s knuckles turn white, her grip on the receiver intensifying. The conversation was brief and one-sided. All T.J. said, was, "Thank you for letting me know."

T.J. walked into her inner office.

"T.J.?" Pearl queried. "What did they say?"

T.J. ignored her, closing the door to her office behind her.

Pearl rushed to the door and pushed it open. T.J. was standing with her back to her, looking out the window to the street below.

"Did you know," T.J. said, "that Scott and I talked about getting a dog? Maybe I'll get one now."

"What did they say?" Pearl insisted.

T.J. turned to face her. "He died, Pearl. They wanted me to make arrangements or contact his family, if he had any." Her face was the color of paste, her lips pinched.

Pearl knew that T.J. was in shock, her rambling on about getting a dog proved that. She left the room and closed the door gently behind her. When she reached her desk she called T.J.'s physician, Doctor Judson. He'd taken care of T.J. since she was a child.

Pearl collapsed in a chair and waited for him. She buried her head in her hands. She had liked Scott. And, T.J.? How was she going to handle his death and the guilt she was feeling for something that wasn't her fault? And the loss! Scott had been more than just a lover, he'd been T.J.'s best friend and stabilizer, in a world that had all but crumbled to dust the day she'd walked out on Jim Westfield.

Chapter Ten

T.J. locked herself up in her hotel room, refusing to see or talk to anyone, even those closest to her. Four days after Scott's death, she was awakened by a pounding on her hotel door. She rolled over in the bed. "Go away," she screamed. "I don't want to talk to anyone."

She hated herself for what must seem like self-pity, but was in realty an onerous sense of guilt she hadn't yet come to grips with.

The pounding finally stopped. "Thank, God," she whispered, and pulled the covers over her head.

A few minutes later they were pulled from her. "What the hell?"

She stared in disbelief at the man who towered over her bed. He was not especially tall, only five-feet-nine. His sandy hair was fashionably long, hugging the back of his neck. Not good-looking in the normal sense of the word, he was attractive in an offbeat way, his nose broken. Normally clean shaven, he had a day's beard on his strong, dimpled chin.

T.J. had broken his nose years ago when a playful exercise had gotten out of hand. She'd blamed herself, but he'd laughed and said, "Forget it. It gives me character."

The intruder was Jim Westfield, her ex-husband, her friend and her lover once upon a time.

"What are you doing here? And how did you get in here?

"The hotel manager let me in. I told him I was your doctor. Hell, you haven't left this room for days. Everyone is worried about you, even the staff here. They all know what happened to Scott. Bad news travels fast." A look of disgust clouded his probing grey eyes. "Look at you! I should have known you'd buckle under real pressure. After all, look what you did to us."

She shot up in bed. She was wearing a pair of Scott's pajamas that she'd retrieved from the clothes dryer that had miraculously survived the fire, as had the garage where it was housed. The garage was the only thing left standing. She'd put the pajamas on in a desperate effort to pull Scott close to her, as if wearing them would bring him back. "What I did to us! That's a good one."

"It's true. I made mistakes, and you're never going to let me forget them."

"Mistakes! That's an understatement. You cheated on me!"

"That's an old argument, T.J. One I can't win. I'm worried about you. You're about to self-destruct again. So, your boyfriend is dead, but you're using his death as an excuse to give up everything you claim to have wanted. You know for a while, I started to believe you might even be good at what you do...or did, until you gave up and crawled into a hole. You're a quitter, T.J. You're going to let Marshall clean up your mess just like he always does."

"That isn't true, and it isn't fair! And I left you, remember?" I went out on my own, made my own way, thank you very much, and I'm damned successful at what I do."

"Then get out of that bed and prove me wrong. Prove that you're made of something worthwhile. If you really loved the guy, find out who killed him. It beats wallowing in self-pity." He shook his head. "And to think I believed I'd lost something when you walked out on me."

T.J. balled her hand into a fist and hit him squarely on the jaw.

He staggered backward and rubbed his chin. "You pack one hell of a punch. That's not what I had in mind when I came here, but it's better than watching you lying around feeling sorry for yourself. Where did you learn to hit like that, by the way?"

T.J. froze, her fist hovering in mid-air. She had a sudden insight. Jim hadn't come here of his own volition. He'd been asked to come here! Only one person had the power, the gumption or the nerve to ask that of Jim. Marsh! He'd known that sending Jim here was the only way to get her mad enough to want to fight back.

She started to tell Jim what she knew to be true, but he was already halfway out the door. "There were times when I hated Scott for waking up beside you every morning," Jim said. "Times when I wanted to call him out. I wanted him out of your life so that I might get back in. I didn't want him out of your life this way." He shook his head. "How can anyone have a chance with you ever again after this?" Then, he was gone.

* * *

Marsh was on the phone when T.J. entered the squad room. She took the receiver from him and set it back in its cradle. "What are you doing, T.J!" he yelled.

"Interfering with your life like you interfere with mine. You sent Jim to see me, didn't you?"

"I don't know what you're talking about."

"Like hell you don't."

Marshall sighed then grinned resignedly. "It looks like it worked. Anyway, it wasn't all my idea. Jim called me when he heard about Scott. He wanted to know if there was anything he could do. He was afraid to call you. He knows how you feel about him." He paused. "Or, how you think you feel about him."

A muscle twitched in her cheek. "Don't play God, Marsh. Not with my life."

"Okay. But he's changed, T.J. I admit, I never liked the son of a bitch much, especially after you married him and he became a big shot lawyer and a womanizer. But when you left him, it took some of the cockiness out of him. It took guts for him to come to you not knowing how you'd react." He grinned. "How the hell did you react, anyway?"

T.J. kicked at his leg. "Just like you knew I would. He made me furious, just like you knew he would. I want my case back, Marsh. I want to find David Sinclair, Michael Sinclair, too, if he's really alive. And I want to find whoever tried to kill me, and killed Scott instead."

Marshall nodded. "Thought you might. I transferred your files back to Pearl this morning. She and Gregg are going over them now."

She bent down and kissed his cheek. "Bless you for caring. What would I ever do without you?" Her eyes sparkled dangerously. "But, if you ever do something like that to me again, I'll kill you."

* * *

Pearl and Gregg looked up as T.J. pushed open the office door. T.J. gave Pearl a knowing look. She'd wager money that Pearl was in on Jim's visit along with Marsh. She crooked her finger at the two of them. "You two. In my office. Now."

Smiles passed between Pearl and Gregg as they followed T.J. into her office.

"All right," T.J. said. "Let's go over what we know so far."

Gregg grinned. "Right," he said. "But, before we do, I have something I want to say. I've been thinking over your offer to join you. I'm going to do it. I'm tired of playing lone ranger."

T.J. gave them both a long hard stare. "Sit down, both of you. You're not coming in with me, Gregg, though I appreciate the gesture. I don't need babysitting, and you're much too good an investigator to live in anyone's shadow, and you like doing your own thing. As for you, Pearl, I don't need mothering, nor do I need chicken soup. I admit I went off track, but I'm back now. Do we all agree, so far?"

They nodded. There were tears in Pearl's eyes, admiration in Gregg's.

Gregg slapped the side of his leg with his hand. "Let's go over everything from the beginning. You start."

T.J. got up from her chair. "Let's begin with Joanne. She's a misfit, a wealthy, lonely misfit who attracted one man because she was rich, and the other...well, who knows. She claims she and David were in love. I believe her. At least I believe that she believes it. Both men left her. One supposedly drowned, but there's reason to think he didn't. Then, there's David Sinclair. Is he dead? I'm beginning to think so. A man followed me to London. Why? To find out what I learned, or for something more sinister? Two attempts were made on my life. Both failed." She swallowed. "Scott died instead of me."

She held up her hands. " I'm all right. What happened to Scott is a bitter pill to swallow, but I'll learn to live with it. What I won't do, is let his death go unanswered. Pearl, the information you were able to pirate from Interpol about the Sinclair brothers? Any more to it than I already know?"

Pearl shook her head. "Only that they're still trying to find David Sinclair just like we are. They never closed their books on him. They could be looking for him even harder than we are."

T.J. looked grim. "I doubt it. Gregg?"

"I checked the airlines and tried to follow the trail of the guy who boarded the plane to London. All I found out was that a man answering his description bought a ticket on first class just hours before the flight. I still think it was Michael Sinclair."

"Why would he do it?"

"Maybe he was in touch with David Sinclair and Joanne didn't know it. Maybe they planned to drive Joanne nuts together."

T.J. looked thoughtful. "I considered that. But what would it gain either of them? And, if it were true, it would mean a conspiracy that was designed to last nine years."

"Charlton Hayward?"

"I considered that, too."

"And?"

"It's all we've got. Pearl, get me on a flight to New York tomorrow."

"I'm coming with you," Gregg said.

T.J. smiled. "Thanks. I was counting on it. Make those two tickets to New York, Pearl."

* * *

T.J. hadn't let Charlton Hayward know she was coming. When she entered the outer office the same uptown receptionist stood guard. This time there was no welcoming smile when she saw T.J.

"Mr. Hayward isn't expecting you, is he?"

"Hardly," T.J. said.

"He's with someone," the receptionist offered.

"We'll wait."

The receptionist was torn. Should she buzz her boss and risk his anger at the interruption, or should she dash in there and warn him as his client was leaving?"

T.J. felt a brief moment of pity for the woman's predicament.

Twenty minutes later the door to Hayward's office opened. A portly man in his late fifties was shaking Hayward's hand. "Thank you, Mr. Hayward. I feel a whole lot better now that I have you on my side."

The receptionist, T.J. and Gregg, moved forward at the same time. The receptionist had the first word. "I tried to tell them Mr..."

Charlton Hayward smiled, seemingly undaunted. "Miss McCall? You should have told me you were coming to New York. As it is, I have a busy schedule. Maybe, later? Dinner, perhaps?"

"No, that would be too easy. You'd try to sidetrack me. I'll see you now, Mr. Hayward."

Hayward glanced over at Gregg.

"He's with me," T.J. said.

"I thought you worked alone."

"I did. I do. Recent events make having someone with me seem prudent."

Hayward displayed exasperation. He looked down at his watch. "All right. Jessica," he said, addressing the tall receptionist. "Cancel my next appointment." And to T.J. "Come on in."

Inside his office, Hayward took a seat in his oversized chair, motioning T.J. and Gregg to the two chairs in front of the desk. He reached inside a mahogany box inlaid with marble for a cigar, and lit it. Blowing smoke, he asked, "Now, what brings you here, and in such a hostile mood?"

"You, me, Joanne, a man that followed me to London, attempts on my life, the death of...the death of a very close friend."

"What are you talking about? You were hired to find Joanne's husband. What you're describing sounds like the plot of a B movie."

"That movie is my life, Mr. Hayward. And you're right, this should have been a simple missing person's case. Somehow, Joanne made it different. And, so, I think did you."

"Explain yourself."

"Gladly. Allow me the liberty of thinking out loud. When I left your office the last time I was in New York, only four people, maybe five, if you count Joanne, knew what my itinerary was. You, me, my assistant, Pearl, and Gregg. I'd trust Pearl and Gregg with my life." She smiled over at Gregg. "I boarded a plane to London in first class accommodations, arranged by you. I was originally booked on coach. A short time before the plane left, a man bought a ticket on my flight, also in first class. He followed me to London."

"Why would anyone do that?"

"You tell me. That same man went to the boarding school after I left there. I think he was sent by someone. I think it was you."

"Why would I do that?"

He was cool, T.J. gave him that. Then that was his stock in trade. "I know it sounds bizarre, especially since I think the man who followed me to London was Michael Sinclair."

"Michael Sinclair is dead."

"Maybe. Maybe not."

"Even if what you're saying is true, and it's preposterous, if I had hired someone to follow you, it wouldn't have been Michael Sinclair. First of all, he is dead, and even if he weren't, I despise the man."

She had to admit her theory had weak spots. "Stay with me, if you will. Whoever hired the man to follow me, may have also hired the same man to run me off the road, and set my house on fire."

"And you think I did all this?"

"Yes, I do."

"But, why?"

"To stop me from finding out that you were part of an elaborate plan to have Joanne declared insane, and take control of the Kirkland billions."

Hayward gritted his teeth. His sudden, well-controlled anger surprised T.J. "I'm a rich man, Miss McCall."

T.J. nodded to Gregg. He took over. "I checked your finances, Mr. Hayward. Sure, you're wealthy, but most of your assets are on paper, and most of those assets are in the name of your corporation. To get your hands on large amounts of money without dissolving that corporation, would be impossible, and, if you dissolved the corporation, the tax consequences would be horrendous."

Hayward nodded. "True, I live very well." His face contorted with anger. "As for the notion that I'd be a party to declaring Joanne insane, it's ludicrous. I saw what three years in that institution did to her. I watched her doubt her own sanity. It made her unsure, and it made her weak. It set her up for the likes of a Michael Sinclair. I vowed after she got out of the institution to see that she never spent one more moment in a place like that."

T.J. was taken aback. His vehemence was overwhelming. He was either the best actor in the world, or he was speaking the truth.

The intercom buzzed him.

"Urgent call for Miss McCall," the receptionist's voice rang out over the intercom. "It's a Detective Hollings."

Hayward pushed a button on the phone and handed the receiver to T.J. She took it. "Yes, Marsh. What is it?"

"New complications, T.J. A body just floated ashore on the beach ten miles from Joanne Sinclair's house. The body's been chewed on, and it's been in the water for a few days. We hope to have an I.D. in a few hours, but we think its David Sinclair."

Chapter Eleven

T.J. took the first flight back. Hayward insisted on accompanying her and Gregg, and T.J. made no objection. There were still a lot of questions she wanted answers to, answers that only he and Joanne had. If the body that had washed up on the beach was indeed David Sinclair, T.J. expected little or no help from Joanne.

She had been in such a hurry to get back that she hadn't asked Marshall how the man who had washed ashore had met his death. It was one of the first questions on her lips when she arrived at the station house. Hayward was close behind her.

"Do you have an I.D., Marsh?" she asked.

Marshall nodded. "Sure do. It was the body of a dead man."

"I'm not in the mood for games, Marsh. Who was it?"

"I mean it was the body of a man previously presumed dead. It was Michael Sinclair."

T.J. swallowed. "How long had he been in the water?"

"A few days. Dead for four days, so the coroner says."

"Then he didn't drown nine years ago!"

"Only if he reincarnated himself as a recent corpse." His tone was caustic.

"An accident?"

"Only if you count bullets as an accident. He was shot in the head, the heart, and," he paused, "and twice in the groin."

Hayward stepped forward. "Does Joanne know?"

Marsh looked over at T.J., a question in his eyes. "Sorry, Marsh," she said. "You two haven't met. This is Charlton Hayward."

Marshall raised an eyebrow. "Is it now? What are you doing here, Counselor?"

"You called Miss McCall at my office. Naturally, when I thought the body was David's I was concerned about Joanne."

"And, now?"

"I'm even more concerned. We thought Michael was dead. When his body was never recovered, Joanne suffered greatly. The press was relentless. There was talk that she and Michael weren't the most happily married couple."

"Talk?"

"All right, the rumors were based on fact, but that didn't make it any easier for Joanne. She blamed herself for Michael's death. I mean his supposed death. They'd argued fiercely the night before he...before he disappeared, just hours before he left for the lake. She never saw him alive again."

Marshall leaned back in his chair. "Now, there we have a little difference of opinion, you and I. You say she saw him last, nine years ago. But, a man claiming to be Michael Sinclair phoned her not so long ago, and may have been placing calls to her for months."

"Phone calls, Detective, from a prank caller claiming to be Michael."

"That isn't all of it. We have reason to believe she met with him recently. The day he died, in fact."

"That can't be!"

"We have evidence to the contrary. True, she lives in an isolated area, but, as luck would have it, a delivery boy from town was dropping off groceries to the Sinclair house four days ago, at exactly the same time that a car pulled up in the driveway. The delivery boy saw a man get out of the car. The kid told us that Joanne seemed distraught when she opened the door to him, and saw the man getting out of his car. Said she acted like she'd seen a ghost. He identified the body as that of the man he saw in her driveway. I was on my way out to question her when you guys walked in. She's a murder suspect now."

"Based on what grounds?" Hayward exploded.

"It's circumstantial, I know, but we have enough to hold her. You're welcome to come along, of course. She'll need a lawyer." He waved a folded piece of paper in Hayward's face." This is a search warrant for her place. We're looking for a twenty-two pistol. What do you bet we find one? I'll pull up every tree if I have to."

"To find a gun?"

Marshall sighed. "That, and maybe a fresh grave, the grave of David Sinclair." Marshall looked over at T.J. "Sorry, T.J., I hate to say I told you so, but I asked you to walk away from this one."

* * *

The room seemed crowded. There was Joanne, Marshall, T.J., a woman police officer, and there was Hayward.

A uniformed police officer entered the room. He was holding a gun by the trigger with a pencil. The gun was wet.

"Now, what do we have here?" Marshall said. "I'd say it was a .22. Where did you find it?"

"Hidden in the toilet tank," the officer said.

"Well, well. I'm going to have to arrest you, Mrs. Sinclair." He nodded at the female officer. "Read the lady her rights."

The police woman's words became a dull drone. "You have the right to remain silent..."

T.J. stared over at Charlton Hayward. He had lost his normal composure and his arrogant self-assurance. His face had turned an unhealthy shade of grey. He looked his age, and then some. He really cares about her, T.J. thought. All that did was confuse her. Hayward was the villain in this thing somehow, wasn't he? Well, wasn't he? She'd been so sure of that when she'd set out for New York to confront him.

Joanne seemed to be the only one in the room who was truly complacent. She's in shock, T.J. thought. What else would make her appear almost serene at a time like this?

"You'll want your lawyer to accompany you, I assume," Marshall said to her.

Joanne moved toward Hayward. "I guess I will. Charlie? Seems like I need you again."

He took a step backward. "I can't, Joanne. I'm a corporate lawyer. A damned good one, but still just a corporate hack. You're being accused of murder." He shivered. "Ridiculous, I know. You couldn't have killed Michael. You couldn't kill anyone."

"Then you'll get me off, Charlie." Her smile was benign. She showed no sign of fear.

"You're not listening, Joanne. I'm not the right man for you, but I'll get you a lawyer who is."

"All right." Once again she was calm, untroubled. She turned to Marshall. She put out her hands. "Are you going to handcuff me?"

Marshall was just as bewildered as T.J. at Joanne's serenity. He cleared his throat. "I don't think that will be necessary."

"Thank you." She turned her attention to T.J. "Will you keep on looking for David? I didn't kill him. They won't find him here on the grounds."

T.J. believed her without reservation, and wondered how she could be so sure. She just knew that she was sure. "I don't know, Joanne, it's a police matter now. You have to concentrate on your defense. If you're innocent, you have to prove it."

"I know. That's why I want you to find David for me. I don't trust anyone else." She flushed. "Except you, Charlie. Will you look for him, T.J.?"

T.J. looked at Marsh, at Charlton Hayward, then back at Joanne. "Of course, I will."

"Then I'm ready to go, Detective," Joanne said.

Joanne left behind her two very concerned people, T.J. and Charlton Hayward. They exchanged glances.

He spoke first. "Well, I'd better be looking into a lawyer for Joanne."

"You surprised me, today, Mr. Hayward. You're either a man who cares deeply for Joanne, or you're one hell of an actor. But, I'm warning you, I'm not through with you yet."

He smiled for the first time since Marshall's phone call to his New York office. "I'd be disappointed in you if you were, Miss McCall. I won't be hard to find. I'm staying in town until Joanne is cleared. I'll call you when I find a hotel."

* * *

Joanne was booked without immediate fanfare, but the anonymity of the arrest was short lived. Within hours, news of her arrest was broadcast and biographies of her wealth, background, and the supposed drowning of a husband nine years ago who she was now accused of killing recently, was a top TV news story and front page material.

T.J. went to see Marshall at his home. His wife answered the door and discreetly left T.J. and Marshall alone.

Marshall lit a cigarette, ignored T.J.'s look of disapproval and took a seat on the couch and placed his feet on the coffee table. "You should have walked on this one, T.J. I think maybe the broad is guilty."

T.J. managed a smile. "I know you do, Marsh. You could be wrong."

"Or, I could be right."

"Were there any prints on the gun?"

"Still waiting to hear. The gun's been in water for days. Don't expect to get any."

"Tough break for you. A good one for Joanne."

Marshall smiled. "Even as a kid you always tried to see the bright side of things. We found her gun in her house, in her toilet tank. It wasn't exactly in plain sight."

"And she had forty acres to hide it on, or a whole damned ocean. It's just too pat, Marsh."

He nodded. "Could be you're right. Then again, she could have expected to get away with it. Could have never thought we'd arrest her. Could have happened that way."

"But you're not sure, are you, Marsh?"

He set his feet on the floor. "Until someone or something better comes along, yeah, I'm sure."

The phone rang twice. Marshall's wife poked her head around the kitchen door. "It's for you, Marsh. The Captain."

Marshall picked up the phone on the end table by the couch. "Yeah. I see. You know why? Really! She's here now. I'll tell her."

He set the receiver back on the cradle. He ran his fingers through his hair and stroked his chin.

"What is it, Marsh?"

"Joanne Sinclair has gotten herself a lawyer."

"What makes that so newsworthy? You expected her to get a lawyer."

"Sure I did. Thought it would be Hayward in the end, seeings as how he's handled the Kirkland business for years, and all of her other affairs.

T.J. admitted she had also expected Hayward to take Joanne's case, despite his protests. "Who did Hayward get? A high-powered New York criminal lawyer, no doubt."

Marshall shook his head. "Nope. Joanne Sinclair got herself a local boy. One of the best."

"Who?" But T.J. already had a feeling of dread.

"I think you know the answer to that, T.J. You've got that look. Same look your father used to get when he was one step ahead of the rest of us, which was often. Hayward just hired Westfield to defend Joanne Kirkland."

Chapter Twelve

T.J. stared at Marsh in disbelief. "Jim is Joanne's attorney! It's a joke, isn't it?"

"Wish it was T.J."

"But who...?"

"Hayward, indirectly, but it was Jim who made the first move. He heard that Hayward was looking for a criminal lawyer and offered his services. Apparently, Hayward liked the idea of local representation. Probably figures it will make the Sinclair woman look less guilty. Smart move, really."

"And who would expect less than that from the great Charlton Hayward?" T.J. said, her voice laced with bitterness.'

Marshall didn't reiterate that the initial move had come from Jim himself. "What are you doing to do about it, T.J.?"

"Not what you and Jim expect or Hayward expects. I'm not going to quit this case."

A grin spread across Marshall's face. "They underestimated you, Honey. So did I, for that matter. Should have known better."

"Yes, you should. Ever since Joanne walked into my office, I've been told to quit, wanted to quit, or been intimidated to quit. But I'll be damned if I will."

"Spoken like your father's daughter. I have a break for you, by the way. A friend of mine, well, not exactly a friend, more like an acquaintance, worked for the CIA until a few years back. I was going to talk to him about the Sinclair brothers. Want to come along?"

It was a hell of a concession, she knew, one she suspected was intended to take her mind off of Jim, and his involvement with

Joanne. An involvement that would place him and T.J. in close contact.

She willingly grabbed at the straw Marshall was extending. "You bet your life I do."

* * *

Tim Clancy was sixty years old, a medium sized man, with non-descript features, medium brown hair and eyes. He had been perfect for his past career.

Marshall introduced him to T.J. in the small, slightly cluttered living room of the older frame house that Tim Clancy now called home.

Clancy took her hand. "You're awfully pretty to be a private cop." He smiled. "Maybe that's why you're so effective."

"You're assuming I am effective."

He shook his head. "I never assumed anything in my life. Not since I entered the company, anyway."

"The CIA?"

He nodded.

Marshall took charge, motioning T.J. to a chair. "I appreciate your help, Tim. Can you tell us what you know about Michael and David Sinclair?"

"Not a hell of a lot about Michael. I understand he turned up dead recently. David was always our concern. Michael was brought in, in an effort to coerce David to work with us, instead of everyone else."

"Was he successful?" Marshall asked.

"Either that, or David Sinclair got tired of dodging us. A deal was cut."

"Are you free to tell us about it?"

Clancy shrugged. "Under the circumstances, I suppose so, just so long as I don't name names. In exchange for identifying several key classified secret brokers, David, through his brother, agreed to accept immunity, and a new identity. The FBI was bought in, and David disappeared into the witness protection program."

T.J. interrupted. "I don't understand, Mr. Clancy. David used his real name when he met Joanne."

"I was getting to that. David Sinclair turned up missing. His new identity, Jerry Crandall, that is, turned up missing. The FBI had placed Sinclair in Quebec. They kept tabs on him, and so did we. One day he didn't show up for work, or at home. Time passed, and we assumed that someone had discovered his new identity, where he lived, and that they took him out. The CIA and the FBI pretended to close their files on him but continued to hope he'd surface, dead or alive. Then, according to you, young lady, he just up and shows himself, runs off with an heiress who can hardly be called a nonentity, and then disappears again." An angry tic pulsed in his cheek. "It just doesn't figure."

None of it did, T.J. readily conceded. David Sinclair was all things to all people. To Joanne he was a saint, to the authorities a rogue and a possible traitor, and to his brother...just what was the relationship between the two men?

"David Sinclair tried very hard not to be seen, Mr. Clancy," T.J. said. "He stayed in the background, used a new name, and was never seen publicity with Joanne, except by a chosen few, like Charlton Hayward. I think the house in the country was chosen as a hideaway."

As the words left her lips, T.J. thought, Hayward again! It always came back to him. She had to talk to him, and this time she wouldn't be satisfied until she believed that she'd ferreted out all there was to know about Joanne, Michael, and David.

* * *

Hayward was staying at the Classic Inn, the most expensive and prestigious hotel the area boasted. The desk clerk rang his room, announced her, and she was escorted up to his room by a bellman. T.J. noted that Hayward had the best accommodations the hotel had to offer.

He opened the door to the bellman's knock. He wore a smoking jacket with a white silk shirt underneath, and black pants. He looked both dashing and at the same time haggard. It proves, T.J. thought, that though the clothes may make the man, they can't mask feelings.

"I've been expecting you," he said, as she was ushered inside. He moved to a fully stocked bar in the spacious living area of the sumptuous suite. "What can I get you?"

"How about some truth?"

He poured himself a straight bourbon, and for her a glass of wine. "As I remember it, wine is your drink."

She took the glass he offered. "No truth, then?"

He seated himself in an easy chair, encouraging her to do the same. "Just what kind of truth is it you think I have, that I haven't already given you?"

"Better yet, Mr. Hayward, what have you told me that if not a lie, is at best a detour away from the truth?"

He signed. "It's obvious that you believe me to be guilty of something, I just don't see what it is you think I've done."

"We could start with Joanne, because somewhere, somehow, I know she's the key to everything. Just how relevant was that incident at the school as to how it shaped her life afterwards?"

"You're very intuitive, Miss McCall. And as competent as I'd heard you to be. Joanne went to that school in England feeling insecure and unwanted. Whatever happened there enhanced that insecurity, and it made her doubt anything she ever did after that. Everything that is, except letting David into her life."

"And you still maintain you don't know what happened to her in England?"

"I swear it on my life, and on Joanne's life."

"You care for her a great deal, don't you? More than as a friend. Are you in love with her, Mr. Hayward?"

He rose up out of his chair, spilling amber liquid on the plush white carpet. "You're disgusting. But I suppose that's a requirement for people in your line of work. You have to think the worst of people. I love Joanne, yes, but like a daughter. Now, if you're quite through..."

"I've only just begun. I'm sorry if I offended you, but it was a logical assumption. Incidentally, I believe you."

He took a seat again. "Thank you." He gave her a shrewd look. "You're a hard case, Miss McCall."

She thought about Scott. About hiding out for almost four days after he died. She laughed inwardly. Sure, she was one hard case. Out loud, she said, "I'm just doing the job I was hired to do. Just how much to you know about David Sinclair, and how much did you know about Michael? I assume you had them both investigated."

He nodded. 'Yes. Michael had done and been many things before he met Joanne. He'd been a waiter, a realtor, an actor, a would-be artist. Many things."

"You left out the part about him working for the CIA for a while."

He was lifting the glass to his lips. He almost spilled the contents.

"The CIA?"

"Oh, come now, Mr. Hayward. I'm just a mere P.I., and you're a powerful lawyer with powerful connections. If I can find out something like that, you have to have known about it."

He got up out of the chair. He went to the bar and fixed himself another drink. "Michael's involvement with the CIA was short-lived."

"And, David?"

"You know about him, too?"

"Parts of it. I know that he was on the CIA's hit list before they converted him to an informant. What I don't know, is why, if you knew all about him, that you let Joanne become involved with him.

In so many ways he was worse than Michael Sinclair ever thought about being."

He returned to his chair. He seemed more relaxed now, on surer ground. "That's true. For Joanne, David was gentle, he was caring, and he made her feel special. If I had told her about his past, it wouldn't have made a difference, because she wanted him in her life. Having him became an obsession. She was happy, I mean truly happy for the first time. She felt like she was worthwhile. I couldn't shatter that dream. It was all she had."

"So you never told her about his past?"

"No."

"The house in the country, the new identities? Your idea, or Joanne's?"

"Hers, but I didn't resist it. Maybe I should tell you..." he emptied his glass. "Can I get you another glass of wine?"

She leaned forward in her chair. "No, I'm fine. What should you tell me?" Her tone was urgent.

"I was going to compliment you on your investigative talents, that's all."

But T.J. knew that wasn't it at all. She also knew that the closed expression on his face precluded getting the real answer to her question.

"You had me followed to London. Why?"

"I've already told you that I didn't."

"And I don't believe you."

"Suppose, and I said just suppose, I did have you followed. Might it not have been in the nature of a protective gesture?"

"Protective! You dare to suggest that having me followed was protective! I felt violated. I think the man who followed me to London was Michael Sinclair. I think that same man ran me off the road and tried to kill me. I think..." her voice quivered. "I think that same man set fire to my house and killed the man I was living with."

"You can't be sure of that."

She rose and stood over him, negating the fact that he was inches taller than she. "You, bastard. I came here thinking that it was only a possibility that you had me followed. Now, I'm convinced of it. I'm calling the police, and I'm going to turn you in."

He pushed her away and prodded her back into her chair. "Listen to me, Miss McCall; you have no proof of anything. If, what you are saying is true, the only one who could prove it is Michael himself, and he's dead. All right, I admit I did have you followed to London. But that's all I'm guilty of. I was as anxious as you were to find out what happened to Joanne in England."

She stared up at him. "I would have told you anything important that I discovered!"

"I couldn't be sure of that."

"And just who the hell did you have follow me?"

He looked away from her. "Anything I did, I did for Joanne."

"Who was he?" She insisted, her lips pursed.

"All right. All right. It was Michael."

Her mouth dropped open. "It was Michael?" Suspecting the identity of the man on the plane and vocalizing those suspicions hadn't prepared her for the truth.

He took the almost empty glass from her hand. 'Let me get you another one." He returned to her side a moment later with her glass full. "Understand this," he said as he handed the glass to her, "I will not repeat, admit, or claim knowledge of what I'm about to say to you, and you have no proof of anything. It goes back over nine years. Michael was making Joanne's life a living hell. She'd threatened to file for divorce, but she couldn't make herself do it, and Michael had a gravy train he wasn't about to give up without a fight. He was living in luxury, and he had a woman for every night of the week, flaunting his infidelity in her face. Joanne, despite my advice, wouldn't cut off his too generous allowance. It was a vicious circle that had to be broken. He had to be made to leave her."

"You bought him off?"

"Yes."

She was more than interested, she was fascinated. "Why fake his death?"

"Because Joanne had to believe that he was totally lost to her. The only way she could do that was if he were dead."

"You arranged his accident?"

"Yes, and I supported him financially until the day he died."

"Why, him? Why send him to London? Why not someone else?"

Hayward let out a mirthless chuckle. "He was the one person I could trust to do it. As long as I continued to support him, he would never betray me."

"You really are a bastard. And you just gave yourself one hell of a motive for murder."

"I didn't kill him."

"Just like you didn't pay him to kill me?"

He sighed. "I didn't do that either. I never heard from Michael when he returned to New York. In fact I assumed he'd double-crossed me and stayed in England. I never talked to him again after I asked him to follow you to London."

Questions, so many questions. "Did you know that he'd been calling Joanne for months?"

"No, I didn't."

T.J. didn't believe him. "It's incredible. You lived a lie, and worse, you let Joanne live a lie, and you almost turned her into a bigamist. How did Michael react to the fact that Joanne took up with his brother? She and David were never married, you know."

He nodded. "Not on paper, anyway. I never told Michael about David. I also didn't tell him where Joanne was. I lied, and said she was in Europe. Yet, if your Detective Hollings is to be believed, a delivery boy saw Michael at Joanne's house. How did he find her?"

"You led him to her."

"I would never do that."

"Not intentionally, maybe. But what was to stop him from following me? He did it once. You probably led him to Joanne through me."

His face turned gray. "I never thought..."

"If I'm to believe you, you never thought much about anything. You may be one hell of a lawyer, but you're a lousy conspirator. You played God with Joanne's life, and you played God with mine, and I won't rest until I see you pay for that." She held up her hands. "I know, I know. I have no proof. Not yet, anyway."

She was almost to the door, when she turned back to face him. He no longer seemed like a giant. He was pathetic, and he was sickening. "The lawyer you retained to defend Joanne? Do you know who he is?"

Hayward frowned. "I know of him. He's had an impressive number of successful cases. He's a real comer, so I hear."

"Oh, yes, he's a real comer, all right. I should know. I was married to him."

It pleased her to see that she had made a deep and worrying impression. Chalk one up for me, she thought. And, having had that thought, she wondered how she could turn Jim's representing Joanne into a weapon against Hayward.

Chapter Thirteen

T.J. was in her new living quarters, a downtown apartment she'd rented until her house could be rebuilt, which might take months. Her phone rang. It was after 9 p.m. Marshall was on the other end of the line.

"Thought I should be the one to tell you, T.J., the evidence against Joanne Sinclair is looking significant."

"What have you got, Marsh?"

"A fingerprint. The house was clean. So, clean, that at first we didn't find any prints except Joanne's. But then we came across one on the front door. It belonged to Michael Sinclair. So, now we know he was there."

"I thought you already had proof of that from the delivery boy."

"A good cop is a good bluffer, T.J., you should know that. The delivery boy did I.D. the body as Michael Sinclair's, the same man he saw at the Sinclair house. With a little prodding from us, of course. You have to remember, the body had been in the water for days, and something had gnawed on it. Small shark, probably. It wasn't a pretty sight. The kid upchucked all over the morgue floor. A good attorney and she has one, will chew the kid up and spit him out on a witness stand."

Using the delivery boy was borderline police ethics, but T.J. was not naïve enough to believe it didn't happen. Her father used to talk about it occasionally. "When you know you have the bad guy," he'd said as he put out his cupped hands, "and keeping his ass for prosecution means stepping over that line just a little bit, I'll walk it, T.J., and I won't lose sleep over it." She hadn't questioned his logic, because she not only loved him, but he'd taught her the importance of a victim's rights. Like her father, and because of him, she believed that too many criminals escaped punishment through technicalities.

"Thanks for calling, Marsh. I'm going to see her tomorrow. You haven't dug anything else up, have you?"

"You mean like David Sinclair's body? No, not yet. But we did find something at her place. We found a car covered up with dead pine branches. It was a dark late model Cadillac. The car is registered to a David and Joanne Sinclair. It's the car that David Sinclair supposedly left in. It was pretty beat up, like it had been in an accident. It had light blue paint on one side." His tone was ominous. "You're car was light blue, T.J."

* * *

The next morning Hayward was coming down the steps of the County jail as T.J. stepped out of the car. He stopped and waited for her to reach his side. "Good news, Miss McCall, Mr. Westfield and I have arranged bail for Joanne. A million dollars."

It was a mere drop in the Kirkland bucket. "That is good news. I came to talk to her, but maybe I should wait."

"No, please, she'll be happy to see you now. She doesn't belong here, Miss McCall."

"Yes, well then that's what they all say, isn't it? Excuse me, Counselor."

Joanne was brought to a small visiting room by a heavily muscled female deputy. Joanne threw her arms around T.J.'s neck. The gesture took T.J. off guard. She gently pushed her away. "Is it that bad in here?"

Joanne looked around the room. "Here? You mean in jail? No. The people are nice really, but I don't know them."

"Sit down, Joanne. I have to talk to you. There's so much you aren't telling. If I'm to help you, I have to know everything that you know."

Joanne looked confused. "My lawyer said I couldn't talk to anyone."

T.J. flushed. "Your lawyer. You mean Charlton Hayward?"

"No. I mean the new one, Mr. Westfield. He was very insistent about it."

T.J. clenched her jaw. "And did he specifically say not to talk to me?"

Joanne frowned. "No."

"Then I don't qualify. I work for you, Joanne. At least I did." She started to leave.

Joanne stopped her. "Please, don't go. Sometimes I think you're the only one who cares about me. I'm sure that Mr. Westfield didn't mean you." A determined look passed over her face. "And, if he did, I'll just have Charlie fire him."

T.J. sat back down. She placed her hand over Joanne's. "I wouldn't hurt you, Joanne. I want to help you."

"I know that."

"All right. Let's start with Michael. He came to your house?"

Joanne pushed an imaginary hair from his eyes. "I don't know. I'm confused."

T.J. stood once again. I can't do this, Joanne. I can't play the game your way. If you can't be straight with me..."

She grabbed at T.J.'s arm. "Wait! Yes, Michael came to the house."

T.J. returned to her seat. "What happened?"

Joanne's hands trembled. "I was frightened. I thought he was dead. Even after the phone calls, I kept thinking that he had to be dead. Then, there he was, alive, and standing in my doorway."

"Did you kill him, Joanne?"

"No!" We argued. I think I hit him with my fists. He knocked me down. Then he left."

"Who wiped the house clean of prints?"

Joanne looked right at her. "I did. I wanted to wash every sign, every smell, and every sense of him, from the house. I scrubbed everything, even places he'd never been. I was exhausted afterwards, mentally and physically. I went to bed and I slept for hours."

"What exactly do you know about David?"

The sudden change of subject took her by surprise as it was intended to do. "David?"

"Yes, David. What did he do before you met him?"

"It didn't matter. It doesn't matter now."

"Then you don't know much about his life before you met him?"

"Only that I needed him. He was kind, considerate, gentle, undemanding, and he was mine."

He sounds perfect T.J. thought. Too damned perfect, and not the David Sinclair she'd been introduced to through Marsh's CIA friend.

"You never really marred him, did you?"

"We were married."

"Not by any church or magistrate. I checked."

"We marred each other in a private ceremony."

"Witnesses?"

"No. We exchanged our vows in a deserted chapel." Her eyes misted. "It was the most beautiful thing I've ever done."

"You wanted Charlton Hayward to think you were married?"

"Yes."

"He knows better."

A malevolent look clouded Joanne's face. "I should have known."

"Don't hold it against him. Whatever else his faults or his crimes, he cares for you a great deal, Joanne."

Joanne seemed reassured. "Yes, I think he does."

"Enough to kill for you?"

"Kill for me? You mean Michael? No! Charlie didn't kill Michael."

Now was the time to tell her about Charlton Hayward's capabilities. That he had 'arranged' Michael's death. That he had had T.J. followed to London. That he may have been behind the attempts on her life. But she couldn't do it. Joanne had so little to hang onto. Too few people she could trust. Are you so sure?" T.J. asked.

"I'm real sure."

"Then I'll ask you again, Joanne. Did you kill Michael?"

"No."

"Then who do you think did?"

Joanne looked squarely into T.J.'s eyes. And without flinching, she calmly said. "David killed him. He told me so."

* * *

"David told you he killed Michael! You've seen him? When?"

"The night Michael was killed."

Yet you asked me the day you were arrested to keep looking for him."

"Yes."

T.J. flushed angrily. "I don't understand."

Joanne sighed. "David came to me in the middle of the night. His presence wakened me. I had the impression that he'd been standing over my bed for some time."

T.J. struggled to maintain composure and exert patience. "Go on."

"He said he was sorry for leaving me, but that he'd had to go. He said I sent him away."

"Did you?"

"I may have, but if I did, I didn't mean to." She once again pushed back an imaginary hair from her forehead. "Sometimes things aren't very clear."

"Then tell me what is clear. When and how did David tell you that he killed Michael?"

"He said he'd been watching the house, watching over me. He loved me, you know. He said so. He said that he saw Michael drive up to the house, and after I let him in, David crawled through a window. He saw Michael and me arguing."

"What did you argue about?"

"We argued about his pretending to die. Michael said that it hadn't been his idea, it was Charlie's. That Charlie had been paying him all these years to stay in hiding. He said that he'd been in Hawaii until a few months ago." Her expression darkened. "And then he said that David could never love someone like me. He said that my marriage to David was a farce, not because we'd never formally married, but because what David and I had wasn't real. He said that I had deluded myself into thinking that David loved me. I hit him with my fist, and he knocked me down. I ran into my bedroom and closed the door. When I looked out a while later, Michael was gone. I went into the living room. There was blood on the Oriental rug. I replaced it with one like it from another room, and I burned it and buried the ashes, and then I scrubbed the house from top to bottom. After that I slept."

T.J. slammed her fist on the table that divided them. "I'm on your side, Joanne, and I can't begin to buy the package you're selling. Did you know when you burned the rug that Michael was dead?"

"I think I must have, because when David said he'd killed him, I didn't question him about it."

"Where is David now?"

"I don't know. That's why you have to find him."

T.J. took a deep breath. "It's time for some truth, Joanne. David is not the man you seem to think he is." She told her what she'd found out from Marshall's CIA friend. "He isn't a very nice man at all."

Joanne clapped her hands over her ears. "Stop it! I won't listen to your lies."

"They aren't lies, Joanne. Hell, think of it. If what you say is true, and David did confess to killing Michael, then walked out on you...again, but this time leaving you to face a murder charge. That isn't love, Joanne, that's betrayal."

"No! No! No! Go away. You're fired. You don't work for me anymore."

T.J. stood up. "You can't fire me, because I quit. I think you murdered Michael Sinclair, but for what it's worth, I don't think you'll ever be convicted of first degree murder, not if Jim puts you on the stand, and he will, because he's too good an attorney not to."

It wasn't until later T.J. realized that Joanne hadn't seemed one bit perturbed by Charlton Hayward's deception and culpability in Michael Sinclair's bogus death.

Chapter Fourteen

T.J. was edgy, waiting to hear from Jim, because she knew he'd call her sooner or later. When his call came, Pearl put him though to her without so much as a comment, and that in itself was a milestone. Pearl could never resist a jibe, even an affectionate one if the situation warranted it.

Jim, typically, came straight to the point. "You went to see Joanne," he said. "I think we should try to work together on this. After all, we have the same end result in mind. We want Joanne to go free."

"That's pretty damned presumptuous of you. Obviously, Joanne didn't elaborate on our last conversation. I no longer work for her."

"She told me. She also told me she acted in haste. She was released on bail this morning, by the way."

"Good for her, but it makes no difference to me. I'm off the case." T.J. hung up on him.

A minute later Pearl put another call though to her. It was Jim again. "Okay, if you won't help her, then help me."

"Why in the hell would I do that?" T.J. severed the connection.

Thirty minutes later, he came storming though the front door, and strode into her private office. "I hate it when people hang up on me," he declared.

"And I hate people who crash their way into my office without an appointment."

He positioned himself in a chair. "Okay, you win. If you want me to grovel, I will. I need your input." He smiled the same crooked smile that she remembered him using when he wanted his own way.

"I'll spring for lunch," he wheedled. "All you have to do is agree to go with me, and hear me out."

T.J. couldn't resist the chance to keep the upper hand now that she seemed to have it. "Say, please."

He swallowed, took a cigarette from a pack of his pocket, and lighted it. "All right, Goddamn it, please."

When they left the building together, Pearl made no attempt to hide her surprise, nor her disapproval.

Jim chose a small but expensive restaurant nearby. As if they'd never been separated and divorced, Jim ordered for both of them, the way he used to when they were together. It reminded her of that night at Twenty-One, when Hayward had taken charge of the meal. She hadn't minded his high-handedness; but she resented the same treatment coming from Jim.

The waiter brought a bottle of wine. Jim made a production of sniffing the cork, and passing the wine past his palate before he nodded his approval. The waiter filled their glasses. Jim lifted his. "To a better understanding."

T.J. made no effort to raise her own glass. Jim shrugged. "Okay, have it your way."

"What do you want from me, Jim?"

"We used to talk a lot when things were good for us, T.J. I miss those days. I miss bouncing ideas off of you."

"I don't miss it at all."

He inhaled and let his breath out slowly. "You don't give a guy a break, do you? I wish I could turn back the clock and be the man you wanted me to be." And when she didn't respond, he said, "Would it help if I admitted I was a first-class jerk? No? All right, then let's talk about Joanne. What happened at the jail?"

"She didn't tell you?"

"Only that she fired you, and she was sorry about it. She likes you. More importantly, she trusts you."

T.J. allowed the waiter to place her meal in front of her. "Do you think she's guilty?"

"Do you?"

"What I think isn't important."

"But what I think is, right? It seems like we've had this conversation, or one just like it before."

"Back then, you said guilt or innocence wasn't important."

"And that drove you away. I didn't kill those women, T.J."

"No, but you helped to get the son of a bitch off who did."

"One of my many sins you can't forgive. I was only assistant council, yet you still hold me responsible for the murders of those women who died after Cryden was acquitted. They never proved Cryden killed any of them, the initial victims, or the later ones. They didn't even arrest him on suspicion after he was acquitted."

"You could have quit the case," she accused him. "Cryden confessed to the murders, but his confession was inadmissible because he hadn't been advised of his rights. He walked on a technicality, and because of a brilliant defense conducted by you and your mentor, Stewart Beldon."

"I repeat, he wasn't even picked up when the new murders occurred."

"And they never arrested anyone else. The case is still open."

"And unsolved. Ask your friend Marshall about it.' Jim shrugged. "It's too late to be an issue between us now, just like my affairs. Besides, you can't hurt me any worse than you already have."

It was the first time he'd admitted that she'd hurt him. At the time he'd been angry, and so had she, with cause. Their anger had successfully concealed any other emotions. Later, pride had negated any possibility of reconciliation from either side. "Will you get her off?"

"Hopefully." He paused. "Whether she's innocent or guilty. That is what you wanted to hear, isn't it?"

It wasn't what she wanted to hear at all. "Joanne is fragmented. I would think that her best defense is mental incapacity. Michael Sinclair's death seems to have placed her over the edge."

"Hayward won't allow it. He's convinced Joanne to plead not guilty, period."

T.J. understood Hayward's line of reasoning better than Jim could hope to. He hadn't witnessed Hayward's heated refusal to listen to any suggestion that Joanne was mentally deficient. "I thought you were her lawyer on this case," she said.

He frowned. "Pull the knife out of my back T.J. I may be the attorney of record, but Hayward still calls the shots. For now, anyway. When I take the case to court it will be a different story. He can't control me from the gallery, and I intend to keep him there. Is she guilty? I honestly don't know. She had motive, she had opportunity, and she had the weapon. There are weaknesses in the D.A.'s case though, like the delivery boy. I can break the kid on the stand."

"What about the fingerprint they found at the house that belonged to Michael Sinclair?"

"A print on the front door, and none inside? They can't prove she ever let him in."

"And you can't prove she didn't."

"I can try."

He had yet to mention David Sinclair. "She told me she didn't kill Michael," T.J. said.

"And you believed her?"

"I didn't that day."

"And, now?"

"I don't know. Oh, to hell with it. I don't work for her anymore. She told me that David came back, killed Michael, and left her again. It would explain the concealed Cadillac the police found on the grounds. It was the same car that ran me off the road, and David could have been driving it that night. If he was the one behind the wheel, he'd want to hide it, or get rid of it. Marsh said there were no prints on the car. None. David Sinclair is a pro. It fits his profile." She looked disgusted. "Hiding the car on the grounds of the house makes him a real son of a bitch. You know the kind," she added pointedly.

Jim poked at his food with his fork, then raised his eyes to meet hers, ignoring her jab, resisting the chance to remind her that he hadn't left her, it was the other way around. "If she's telling the truth, then you have to help me find him. You can't quit now, T.J. Are you forgetting Scott? Are you forgetting that someone, maybe David Sinclair, tried to kill you? And even if he wasn't the man behind the wheel, whoever it was wins, if you pull out now."

She hated him for being right, and she hated him for invoking Scott's name. "I can't work for her again."

"Then work with me."

"What?"

"I said come work with me. You'll be working for yourself, too. You want to know what really happened, don't you?"

"I can't work with you!"

"Why, not? It'll be an arrangement that will benefit us both. You already have the edge because you've worked this case from the start."

"I know what my value is. What do you plan to throw in?"

"I'll tell you everything I'm doing."

"What if my investigation proves Joanne to be guilty?"

"We'll worry about that if it happens."

T.J. pushed the plate from her. She had barely touched her food. "We want different things, Jim. I guess we always did, I was just slow to see it. It wasn't just your affairs. You want a win, and I want justice. I want justice for Scott, and I want it for me. If I do agree to work with you on this case, I'll take anything incriminating about Joanne I find straight to Marsh. Do you still want me on those terms?"

"I'd want you on any terms. Hell, you're the reason I wangled my way on this case in the first place."

T.J. flushed. He was confusing her. Why hadn't she realized that a part of her would always care for him? Not the way she used to, but damn it, she still cared. "The fact that Joanne is one of the wealthiest women in the country, with a tragic and intriguing background, had nothing to do with it, I suppose?"

"It was the icing on the cake, I admit." Before she could respond, he added, "Since you left me, I haven't found a woman to take your place, and God knows I've tried. You're a hard act to follow."

She refused to meet his eyes, staring down at her plate. "As I recall you found several women to take my place before I left you. But let's skip all that. It's ancient history, like us. We're here to talk about Joanne.

"All right. I'll ask you again. Will you stay on the case?"

"I'll think about it," she said.

They hardly talked on the way back. He dropped her off in front of her building. Riding the elevator upward she thought about all the things she could have said, and now wished she had. She wished she'd told Jim that he was still an arrogant son of a bitch whose first love; no matter what else he claimed, was and always would be the case he was working on at the time, and his need to win it at any cost. Then, she thought about Hayward. She was sure he wouldn't be pleased to hear that she and Jim were working together should she agree to Jim's request.

It was enough of a reason to consider saying yes, to Jim.

* * *

T.J. told Pearl about lunch with Jim and his asking her to work for him. After a pause she added, "He says he wants me back."

Pearl gave T.J. her sternest look. "He always wanted you back, T.J. That was never a secret. You wouldn't'...?"

"Don't worry; it isn't even a remote possibility. Not in this lifetime, anyway."

Pearl continued to look concerned. "Sometimes I wondered, still do every once in a while, what you might feel for him under all that anger. I stopped worrying about it for a while when you met Scott."

It was still painful to hear Scott's name, and especially painful to have reference made to what they'd shared. He'd come along in her life at a time when she was desperately needy. She hadn't married him for a lot of reasons, not the least of which was that she wasn't sure that she wouldn't be using him as a shield against whatever feelings she might have left over for Jim. Now that he was dead, she wished they'd married, and she'd had a child by him, something tangible to let the world know he'd been here and left a small piece of him for her to cling to.

"Sorry," Pearl said. "I didn't mean to hit a nerve."

The hell she didn't!

"Are you going to work for Jim? And, if you say yes, have you thought about how it will be? Can you really work with him?" Pearl asked.

"If I play by my rules, I can." But there was uncertainty in T.J.'s voice.

The office phone rang. Pearl handed the receiver to T.J. "It's that headmistress in England."

T.J. answered with expectancy. "You remembered something, Miss Bramfield?"

"Not exactly," the older woman said. "I...well, I didn't tell you everything."

T.J. tried to remain patient. Everywhere she turned people were withholding something. "Like what?"

"Some of the girls shared rooms at the request of their parents. Joanne was one of those girls. Her parents hoped she'd become less of an isolationist. She shared a room with a girl named Ann Sherwood. I didn't feel at liberty to tell you about her when you were here, but we've just completed a school reunion, and Ann attended it. We had a chance to chat, she and I. I asked her if she'd be willing to talk with you. She said, yes."

T.J. cupped her hand over the receiver. "It's about a possible witness or confidant to Joanne during the time of the incident in England. The timing is bad, but I'll have to go over there. What is Gregg doing?"

"He's checking into the Kirkland background some more, and he's digging into Hayward's past. He left for the East Coast this morning."

"Damn!" T.J. removed her hand from the receiver. "I guess I could catch a flight tomorrow."

"No need, Miss McCall. Ann makes her home in your country now. She lives in Los Angeles. She arrived back there yesterday."

"That's great." T.J. motioned to Pearl for a pen and paper. "Where can I find her?"

"1213 Vinewood. It's a convent."

"Are you telling me she's a nun?"

"Yes, My Dear, she is. Her name is Sister Theodora, now. That's why I was hesitant to talk about the fact that she and Joanne shared a room. I knew that Ann had entered a convent. Even in this day in age, a nun is still removed from life to some degree, don't you think?"

T.J. was a Protestant, and not a devout church goer. She had no way of knowing the answer to Miss Bramfield's question. All she knew for sure was that nuns now wore shorter skirts and longer hair.

"Thank you Miss Bramfield. You can't possibly know how relieved I am to know that she is a nun."

"Why in the world is that?"

"Because," T.J. said, a smile on her face, "this could be the first person I will have talked to since I took this case who is liable to tell me the damn truth."

* * *

The convent was in a run-down neighborhood where little black bodies ran carelessly into the street. There was graffiti on adjoining properties. Only the convent had escaped that slice of vandalism.

Sister Theodora was sent for, and when she appeared, she silently let T.J. into a small bare room that contained only a table and four chairs.

When she spoke, it was with a genteel English accent. "Miss Bramfield seemed to think that I may be able to provide you with background on what happened that night at Granite Hall. I have to admit I'm wondering why it's so important after all these years."

"Did Miss Bramfield tell you why Joanne hired me?"

The nun nodded. "Yes. And I heard about Joanne's first husband. What a tragedy."

"Murder is always a tragedy, Sister. I'm working for Joanne, trying to locate her second husband." There was no point in burdening the Sister with the fact that David and Joanne hadn't officially been wed. T.J. went on, "Working for Joanne has been a challenge that requires I know more about her. No one seems to know her that well, except her attorney, Charlton Hayward, and he isn't telling me much. Do you know what happened that night at the school, Sister?"

"My version is a reasonable assumption only."

"I'll settle for that. Were you and Joanne friends?"

The nun smiled. "No. Oh, we talked. It's hard not to when you share a room, but we were never really friends."

"But you did talk?"

"Yes. She was angry at her parents for sending her away. She couldn't tolerate rejection. I think that's why what happened that night did happen."

"Can you tell me about it?"

"This is difficult for me, Miss McCall. I'm used to keeping confidences, but nothing I'm about to say was said to me in confidence, and the conclusions I'm drawing are strictly my own."

Sister Theodora's face bore no enhanced stress lines, but now her brow creased with worry. "I've carried the events of that night with me for so very long. It's been a burden I've yearned to unload. Will the knowledge of what I believe to have transpired that night help Joanne?"

"I think it will, Sister. It might help me to help her."

"Miss Bramfield thought as much. Like I said, Joanne made no attempt to make friends, and yet I think she would have wanted to if she'd only known how. Miss Bramfield told me that she informed you about her suspicions of a cult within the school's walls."

"Yes. Is it true?"

"In a very childish sort of way. The school catered mostly to the rich and spoiled. Some of the girls were born leaders. The most notable during my time there was a girl named Thelma Scoggins. She led, others followed. She engineered silly little ceremonies in the basement when the teachers were asleep. It was not a serious endeavor. There was a lot of giggling done, and only amateur and very lame attempts at devil worship."

"You attended these sessions?"

"Not attended, eavesdropped. Joanne asked me to sneak into the basement with her on one occasion. I went because she wouldn't take no for an answer."

"And what happened the night of the incident?"

The nun clasped her hands together, as if in prayer. "I have to go back a little to the time when Joanne developed a crush on Hawkins."

"The janitor!"

"Yes. All we girls were assigned little plots of garden to work. I was a natural; my father was a horticulturist at heart. Joanne hated the soil. Hawkins used to help her out so she wouldn't get into trouble. Every seed that was planted in Joanne's little plot was sown by Hawkins."

"That was nice of him."

"He felt sorry for her."

T.J. had had this image of an older man. It was Hawkins dying of a heart attack that had led her to that conclusion. "How old of a man was Hawkins?"

Sister Theodora smiled. "Very old to girls my age, except, of course, to Joanne. She'd spent most of her life around older people. I think she saw him as a father figure at first, and then she fantasized about him in a romantic way. Hawkins was in his thirties. His wife and daughter were dead from some kind of an accident. He was very lonely, I think. Maybe it was that loneliness that gave him and Joanne their bond. I think they recognized a need in each other."

"He returned Joanne's feelings?"

"Not at all. He didn't even see the signs. For him, she was just a lonely child in need."

"Pardon me, Sister, but you were so young at the time. Can you really say you know what Joanne felt, or Hawkins either?"

She nodded. "I think so."

There was much wisdom in the nun's blue-green eyes, and T.J. decided to give her the benefit of the doubt, and to believe her. "I understand there were rumors of rape."

"Yes, there were."

"Could it have been true? After all, a man in his thirties, alone, dealing with the loss of a wife and child, and admired by a rich American girl. It could have happened."

"I don't think so."

"Then please give me your version of that night."

"Joanne had written Hawkins notes. Silly schoolgirl notes. Then she received one from him. I never saw it, so I don't know what it said, but she was violently upset about it. She said, "He's just like all the others who want to throw me away, but he won't get away with it."

"I forgot about the incident," the nun continued, "until that night. Joanne told me she was going to sneak down to the basement again. It had been rumored there was to be a cult meeting. I wanted no part of it. Even then I knew that I wanted to give my life to God. I was no longer amused by Thelma's antics, I was disgusted by them."

"And that night?" T.J. prodded.

"I awoke a little before 2 a.m. Joanne wasn't in her bed. I became worried. The meetings were always over before midnight. I considered awakening Miss Bramfield, but decided against it. I thought that maybe Joanne had fallen asleep in the basement. There would have been hell to pay if she'd been caught." She flushed. "I'll have to say a few Hail Mary's for that lapse. I crept downstairs." She shivered. 'I never will forget what I saw when I got to the basement."

T.J. sat on the edge of her chair. "What did you see?"

"Joanne was alone in there. She was naked. Blood trickled down from her breasts. She seemed almost happy to see me. I started to ask who had done this to her when she pulled a knife from behind her back, and started to nick herself with the point of the blade, again, and again, and again. I opened my mouth to scream, but she placed a bloodied hand over my lips, and then she ran into the night."

"What did you do?"

"I went back to my room. I was terrified. I was afraid to tell anyone about what I'd seen. I have never spoken of it until Miss Bramfield pressed me about that night at the reunion a few days ago. I never saw Joanne after that night. She was placed in the school infirmary, and her parents picked her up in their private jet the next day. Hawkins became embroiled in the incident because they found crumpled up bits of notes in Joanne's trash can. Notes written to Hawkins, but never sent. The aftermath of that night was too much for him to take. I heard that he was questioned relentlessly, and then he lost his job. His work was all he had left after he lost his family. He died shortly afterwards. I've carried the guilt for that, too, and blamed myself, thinking that what happened at the school contributed to his early death. If only I'd had the courage..." her voice trailed. "After he died, there seemed to be no point in coming forward, because like everyone else at the school, I wanted to put that night behind me."

"Your conclusion of that night, Sister? Who do you think abused Joanne?"

"That's the whole point, Miss McCall. I don't think anyone abused her. I believe Joanne inflicted every one of those wounds on herself."

Chapter Fifteen

Much like his last trip back East, this excursion into Joanne's past wasn't getting Gregg anywhere. He suspected that the mastermind behind the wall of silence that he met at every turn was Charlton Hayward. Thus far, he'd managed to ascertain that the Kirkland mansion was no longer staffed by anyone who'd been there during the years that Joanne had lived there. All the domestics who'd been employed during those years that he'd located so far weren't talking. He deemed it no coincidence that all of them lived very well, resided in expensive suburban neighborhoods, drove nice cars, and had fat little bank accounts.

It reeked of a cover-up.

When he was about to give up and return to home base, he got lucky. The last ex-servant on his list, Gertrude McPheron, was delighted to talk to him.

Gertrude McPheron was in her late seventies, her thinning silver hair encased in a mesh net. She was remarkably spry for her age, answering Gregg's knock on her door with quick brisk steps. She'd emigrated from the British Isles in her teens as a domestic, and worked for the Kirkland's from the time she arrived until her dismissal. In contrast to the other ex-servants homes, her small brick dwelling was modest and there were no fancy cars in her garage.

She insisted on bringing Gregg some tea and home-made scones. "Here, My Boy, some scones will put some meat on your bones. To be sure you'll be needing some. 'Tis only the food that I miss now of my native Ireland. I thought some about going back when I was let go, but I'd outlived all my kin, and everyone else I ever knew, and I buried my husband twenty years gone by." Her eyes took on a faraway look. "Ben was the gardener at the Kirkland house. He was a warm and gentle man who worked wonders with all growing things. Put a plant in his hand, and it thrived, and he was a marvel with delicate flowers. The Kirkland's had the best orchids in the state, and a garden fit for royalty, which they were, within their own circles." She quickly returned to full alertness. "Now, you'd better be after telling me what's happening with Miss Joanne. I've been reading some terrible, terrible things." She pointed to a pair of thick bi-focals on the table. "With the help of those infernal spectacles, mind you. 'Tis grateful I am that my mind is healthy, but bits and pieces of my body are in need of modern contraptions." She fondled her earlobe. "Marvelous things these hearing aids. I was reduced to hearing conversations only as whispers before I had this gadget put in, and I got myself one of those metal hip sockets last year." She shook her head. "Spare parts, that's what life is like when you get to be my age, young man. Now, what can an old lady like me be telling you?"

He laughed. "You look marvelous for your age, Mrs. McPheron. You remind me of my grandmother. Like you, I think she'll outlast most of us. I'll tell it to you straight. I don't know what I'm looking for, but you're the only one who ever worked for the Kirklands while Joanne was growing up who is willing to talk to me."

She nodded in a knowing way. "Can't say as how I'm surprised. Damned fools, the lot of them, and greedy, too. They wouldn't know the meaning of the word loyalty unless it had a price tag on it." She winked at him. "Then you'll be after knowing about any dirt that got swept under the rug? To be sure, there was plenty of it, if you had a mind to see it." Her eyes twinkled.

Gregg pulled out a tiny tape recorder. "The woman I work for will want to hear everything you have to say. Do you mind?"

"Not at all, My Boy. And call me, Gertie. Now, where shall I begin?"

* * *

Gregg settled into a chair in T.J.'s office, and placed a cassette tape on her desk. "Finally," he said. "Someone who was willing to talk about the Kirklands. It's all there on the tape."

"Is it reliable?"

He tipped his head to one side and then the other. "Glossed up a bit in places, I suspect, but essentially true, I think." He smiled. "Gertrude McPheron is one of a kind. You should meet her. You'd like her."

T.J. lifted the tape, fingered it, and then put it down. "Can you encapsulate it for me till I get a chance to hear the whole thing?"

"Sure. Gertie was with the Kirklands since she came to this country as a teenage domestic immigrant."

"Gertie?" T.J. said.

"Yeah, Gertie. She insisted I call her that. Gertie started out as a lowly housemaid, and rose to the ranks of housekeeper by the time Joanne's father, John Kirkland, married one Caroline Simms. To hear her tell it, Gertie ran the Kirkland mansion single-handedly." He grinned. "And I wouldn't doubt it. According to her, John Kirkland was a cold fish who was married to the business long before he tied the knot with Caroline. Marriage didn't change his priorities. Caroline Kirkland, on the other hand, was outgoing, at least in the beginning, but as the marriage deteriorated, she became sullen and withdrawn. Gertie told me that Caroline found solace in someone else's arms."

"Really! Please go on. Who did Caroline Kirkland turn to?"

"You'll love this. It was the big man, himself, Charlton Hayward."

T.J. tapped her fingers on the desktop. "The McPheron woman knows this for a fact?"

"Yup. She said she saw them together in a passionate embrace more than once. But there's more."

"I can hardly wait!"

"Gertie said the affair was of short duration. She overheard Caroline telling Hayward it was over, and she said she also overheard John and Caroline arguing the day Caroline told him she was pregnant with Joanne. John Kirkland, it seems, was aware of the affair. Gertie said he didn't seem as concerned about the affair itself, as he was about who fathered the child she was carrying."

T.J. slapped herself on the forehead. "Why didn't I see it? Of course! Hayward has reason to believe that Joanne is his daughter! No wonder he's so damned protective of her, and I accused him of being in love with Joanne!"

"I'd have bought a ticket to see that ," Gregg said. "But it's not so cut and dried. Gertie says that Caroline swore there was no way the child could be Hayward's. A few days later, according to Gertie, there was a showdown between the three of them. Caroline once again denied that Hayward could be the father of her child, but both men it seems chose to believe differently."

" Mrs. McPheron heard all this?" There was amazement and skepticism in T.J.'s voice. "She is one enterprising woman!"

Gregg laughed. "And, nosy. You can say it, T.J. Gertie herself admits to it."

"Yet if what she says is true, Kirkland not only kept Hayward on the payroll, he made him executor of his will."

"To do less would have created a scandal. Hayward was like family. The Kirklands avoided scandal and gossip at any cost. It was probably Caroline's idea to make Hayward Joanne's guardian in case of mental incapacity. The final will was written only days after Joanne was committed to the sanitarium. It was probably John Kirkland's idea to leave everything to Joanne in a life estate. Gertie said the man never so much as gave Joanne a kind word, let alone affection."

"That explains a lot of things. I have a reasonable version of what happened to Joanne in England. I'll tell you about it later. What did Mrs. McPheron have to say about the Sinclair brothers?"

"A lot about Michael. Gertie felt sorry for Joanne. She said she never missed the opportunity to give her a hug. The woman is a saint, but Joanne was too insecure to accept the affection Gertie offered. That's why, Gertie said, Joanne was ripe for someone as suave and conniving as Michael Sinclair. He was a womanizer from the word go. She vocalized her amazement that even someone as naïve and gullible as Joanne could have been taken in for more than a moment, let alone marry him."

"And, David?"

"He was a mystery to her. She never actually met him. She said she heard that someone was staying in the guest cottage, but Joanne gave orders that the occupant was not to be disturbed, nor was the cottage to be cleaned by anyone but herself. Gertie said that in itself surprised her, because Joanne hadn't ever done a day's work in her life. Joanne gave orders that dinner for two was to be left in the oven every night, and the house left unattended by servants after 7 p.m. She said Joanne was adamant about it."

T.J. winked. "But the good Mrs. McPheron wouldn't have let that get in the way of her natural curiosity, right?"

Gregg grinned. "Naturally, not. She says she peeked in the windows of the guest cottage and saw evidence that some one was living there, but she didn't see the man himself. There were men's clothes on the bed, a pipe on the table, and dirty dishes in the sink, and up at the main house, there was the smell of tobacco in Joanne's bedroom. Before she could spy further, Joanne caught her snooping and fired her on the spot. Gertie was flabbergasted. She'd done her best to nurture Joanne since the day she was born to make up for the parental love she was deprived of. John had dismissed Joanne because he believed her to be someone else's daughter. Caroline, on the other hand, blamed Joanne for making her own life a living hell. If John Kirkland was cruel and insensitive to Joanne by ignoring her very existence, his treatment of his wife was even worse. The only thing Joanne's parents had left in common was Joanne's brother, and when he died, any semblance of unity was gone forever."

"She could have left him."

"So she could. She just couldn't leave all that money."

"As per Mrs. McPheron again?"

Gregg nodded.

"What else did your Mrs. McPheron say?"

"She appealed to Hayward about her dismissal, but he wouldn't overrule Joanne."

"Did he seek to pay off like the others?"

"She was pensioned off, but no, he never asked her not to talk. He probably knew it wouldn't do him any good."

T.J. looked thoughtful. "Ever since I became involved in this case he's been waiting for the other shoe to drop. I almost feel sorry for the son of a bitch."

* * *

The office was quiet. Pearl had left an hour earlier. T.J. had no desire to go home. The apartment, though nice enough, would never feel like home, and there would be no one there to greet her. How she missed Scott.

She put the cassette that Gregg had brought her into a tape recorder and sat back to listen. When she was only a few minutes into the tape, she knew why Gregg spoke about Gertrude McPheron with such fondness. Close to the end of the tape, after Gertie had told Gregg about Joanne firing her, Gregg asked, "You must have been resentful after Joanne let you go. You'd done so much for her."

"Resentful? Lordy, no," Gertrude McPheron protested. "When I read about what Miss Joanne was going through, my heart fairly ached for her. I could never wish Miss Joanne ill. Ben and I lost our only baby in the womb. I never had another." She sniffed. "Women today are so lucky today. They plant seeds nurtured in laboratories into a woman's body, and a miracle is born. In my day, you either could have children, or you couldn't. No, I would never wish Miss Joanne ill. I needed that poor pathetic child as much as she needed me. To be sure, the day she gave me my walking papers, I was hurt, and I was upset, but I understood why she'd done it. Miss Joanne had gotten herself another man that she didn't want to share with anyone. Small wonder after the criticism she came under after she brought Mr. Michael into the house. I'd say if she was to be shamed again, she didn't want anyone to witness it. I only went to Mr. Hayward looking to get my job back because I was afraid for her, afraid that she'd gotten herself another man who'd break her heart. Mr. Michael was a poor excuse for a human being. He did her wrong. He paraded all those other women in front of Miss Joanne without so much as a bat of an eye, and many was the time he had one of them share his bed the whole night through. I wouldn't have blamed her if she'd drowned him in that boat he went out in the day he disappeared. Sometimes, I thought she had. If she's done him in now, he sorely needed killing."

T.J. could almost see the frown that was almost surely on the old woman's face, as she continued. "Now, the other one, the brother, that's another story. Seems to me like he's cut from the same cloth, as Mr. Michael. Poor Miss Joanne. She sure can pick em."

T.J. turned off the tape. She was angry with herself. A woman who'd practically raised Joanne, had enough empathy and human kindness to overlook being dismissed after years of service, and T.J. hadn't been able to get past the same defensive treatment. "Now who's the poor excuse for a human being," she whispered to herself.

She was getting ready to turn out the lights and leave, when she looked up and saw Jim standing in the doorway. "You really should lock the door when you work late T.J., anyone could have walked in here."

She picked up her purse. "You're right. Anyone just did."

"Ouch! You always have your claws out around me, don't you? Maybe you should ask yourself why."

"I know why. I assume you came to ask me if I can work with you. The answer is yes, and no. I'll work for Joanne again if she'll let me, and in a way I suppose that puts me in your corner, too."

"What changed your mind about Joanne?"

"Something you'd never understand; the milk of human kindness."

"You want to explain that?"

"Gregg interviewed a woman who was with the Kirklands since before Joanne was born. She shed light where there was darkness, and so did an English nun. I think it's more than possible Joanne killed Michael Sinclair, and in her own mind was able to justify it. You have to plead her case as diminished capacity, Jim. Either that, or prove to a jury beyond a reasonable doubt that Joanne couldn't have done it."

His smile was all-knowing. "I think you can help me with that if it's humanly possible. That day after the fire when I gave you such a hard time, I didn't mean those things I said. I had to shake you loose from the destructive self-pity you were wrapping yourself up in like a poisonous cocoon. You really are good at what you do, T.J." He frowned. "And what was that about a nun? What does a nun have to do with Joanne?"

She stared up at him. "Everything. And don't turn nice on me, Jim, or I might have to re-evaluate the way I think about you." She swept past him and flipped the light switch on her way out the door. "I wouldn't want to do that," she said over her shoulder as she made her way to the front door. "Lock up after you when you leave. You were right. You just never know what might come walking in."

Chapter Sixteen

T.J. called Pearl and Gregg into her office. She was standing with her back to an easel, a black marker between her fingers.

"Sit down," she said. "I called you guys in here so we could brainstorm. Now that I'm back on the case again," she added, "it's time to get down to serious business."

"How did Joanne take your wanting back on the case?" Gregg asked.

"Like a drowning woman. She made me feel rotten about dumping her in the first place." T.J. placed the marker against the surface of the board sitting atop the easel. She made four columns, labeling each separately, and placed a major heading across the top that read: SUSPECTS.

The first column was labeled: JOANNE. The second: HAYWARD. The third: DAVID SINCLAIR and the last was labeled with a large question mark. Off to the side, she had a column labeled: MICHAEL.

T.J. began to write on the board. When she was through, she stepped back. "Joanne is fragmented. "It's not surprising now that we know how little love she's known. If we're to believe the nun's version of what happened that night at the school, then Joanne deliberately abused herself with the intent of implicating the janitor. Did she do it because he scorned her attentions? I think if we believe the nun's premise at all, then we have to take that as a given. Her parents, no doubt, placed Joanne in that institution with more than just concern for her mental health. Her actions in England made her an embarrassment. Like everything else that became a nuisance or an embarrassment, they made it go away. In this case they locked their problems away."

"Do you think Joanne knows what happened at the school and is lying about having blocked it from her mind?" Pearl asked.

"There's one way to find out. I'll ask her. I didn't do it when I told her I'd be willing to go back to work for her, because I wanted this session with you guys first. But yes, I think she knows what happened, and at the very least is practicing denial."

T.J. pointed at a spot on the board labeled: MICHAEL. "Joanne married Michael Sinclair. If she was looking for love from him, she never found it. He, like the janitor, scorned her affections. With him, for whatever reason, she continued to hope that the love she felt would be reciprocated. It didn't happen. Then he supposedly drowned, except now we know he didn't."

T.J. indicated the column that read: DAVID. "Whatever he was to anyone else, he made Joanne feel loved, and by then she must have been desperate for it. Did he have a motive for making her think he loved her, or is it possible that he really did care deeply for her? Stranger things have happened. Only David knows the answer to that question. And he too, left her."

She turned to face them. "Did Joanne kill Michael Sinclair? If not, she must have wanted to after he showed up in her life after nine years of silence. Or did David kill him as Joanne claims?"

She stepped back to the board. "We'll get back to Joanne later." She moved her marker to the second column. "Charlton Hayward, a man of great influence, but with a skeleton in his own past that made him eager to buy into Joanne's. He had an affair with Joanne's mother. Is Joanne his daughter? Caroline Kirkland said, no." She glanced over at Gregg. "That is, if we can put stock in Gertrude McPheron's testimony. And can we? By her own admission she needs glasses and a hearing aid. Can you check and see just when her eyesight and her hearing went bad, Gregg?"

He nodded.

"Good. All along," T.J. went on, "Hayward has been like a mother hen where Joanne is concerned. If he believes, or chooses to believe that Joanne is his daughter, it makes sense. If he cares about her as much as I'm beginning to think he does, would he kill for her? I think the answer to that question is that it's a distinct possibility."

She moved to the third column, viciously stabbing the board with the marker. "David Sinclair. Where the hell is he? He's everywhere, and yet he's nowhere. He's sought by the CIA and the FBI, yet he manages to surface and yet is never discovered."

"Then you think he's alive?" Gregg asked.

"For the moment, I do. He's sure as hell a man of mystery. Each person who knew him paints a different portrait of him. Why, if he wanted to disappear from the CIA and the FBI's clutches, did he choose to link up with a woman whose own past is clouded, and who lived in a fishbowl? Was he hiding in plain sight? And did something spook him that made him leave her? Pearl? Did you get the name and address of his last foster home?"

"I did. It's on your desk."

"Thanks. Did David run me off the road? Did he set fire to my house? Was he afraid that I'd expose him and endanger him? Did he really kill Michael? And, if so, why? Was it because he was madly in love with Joanne? I don't see him with that kind of motive, and I'm not buying his unintentional involvement with the CIA." She looked over at Pearl. "Were you able to get the information I asked you for?"

"Yes, but it wasn't easy. It cost you a lot in coin, and it cost me a night out with an old friend."

T.J. raised her eyebrow. "An old friend? How old of a friend?"

"Old enough. We had a few dinners, and a few laughs when I was with the IRS and he was a government employee. He never said what part of the government he worked for, but I always suspected he was with intelligence. The information is on your desk along with the other stuff you asked for."

"You're a gem."

"What else is new? You didn't hire me because I could type!"

It was true. T.J. had recognized Pearl's value the moment she'd walked into her smaller quarters three years ago. Pearl knew more people in more places than anyone T.J. had ever met, and T.J. had known how valuable those connections would be to an investigative agency. She'd started Pearl out at twice the salary of a secretary or receptionist, the job she'd applied for, to make sure she kept her. And now Pearl's connections were proving to be pure gold.

"What's the fourth column all about?" Gregg asked.

"It's the one suspect that we never considered to be relevant, and it's not a person, but an entity. Who knew more about David Sinclair in his later years than anyone else?"

"Joanne?" Pearl volunteered.

"No. I don't think she knew him at all. I think like Michael, he was using her for his own ends. Michael was just more obvious about it."

"The people he worked for?" Gregg proposed.

"Right. Was he really working for some vague international clients? I think not. I don't think Sinclair was a soldier of fortune who was a thorn in the CIA's side. I think he was CIA trained. Remember Pearl, when you said it was possible they were looking for him even harder than we were? I think you were right."

"I was?"

"I think so. I'm going to have to prove it though. I'll go visit his last foster parents, and then I'm going to pay another call on Tim Clancy.

* * *

Glenn and Irene Roberts were in their late fifties. Life hadn't been easy for them. They'd lost their own two children, one to crib death, the other to cancer. They'd filled their lives with other people's children, and were in fact, still doing it.

Irene Roberts was eager to talk about David. Glenn Roberts was not. He was openly hostile. "Ungrateful little bastard. We didn't have much then, we still don't, but we gave him and the others who were here with him, all that we could spare. Then, one day he just ups and runs off without so much as a thank you."

"What kind of boy was he?" T.J. asked.

Irene Roberts answered before her husband of thirty years could inject more hostility. "He was a good boy underneath; at least I'd like to think so. He was a hard one to fathom. He was fourteen when we took him in. He wasn't the talkative kind. He was secretive, and he was resentful. We thought it might be because the social services had separated him from his brother, so we tried to get Michael, too. We couldn't. We've been reading all about Joanne Kirkland and David. Did they ever find him?"

"Not yet. That's why I'm here. Do you have any idea where he went when he left here?"

"Not a clue," Glenn Roberts answered. "It wasn't because we didn't look or didn't care." He was defensive. "Money was tight, like I said, so we couldn't afford to do much more than worry."

"You'd think you'd get used to it, wouldn't you?" Irene said. "We've seen them come, and we've seen them go. We've always known they weren't ours, that some day someone would claim them, but we never got used to it. David was the only one to ever run away. The others were taken from us when their parents were able to have them back."

"Why do you think he ran away?"

"To find his brother, perhaps? I don't know," Irene said. "I was afraid he'd gotten himself into something he couldn't handle. Two other boys ran off at about the same time. There was talk about a stranger being seen hanging around the school." She shuddered. "You hear such awful things. When we read about Joanne Kirkland and her problems, it was a relief to know that David wasn't dead, at least. He isn't, is he?"

"I don't know yet. About the man hanging around the school? Was he ever picked up?"

Irene held onto her husband's arm. "No. He went away."

T.J. avoided looking at Glenn Roberts, concentrating on Irene instead. She was the one to deal with on an emotional level. "Did he go away at the same time David and the other boys disappeared?"

Irene clutched her husband's arm tighter. "Yes."

131

It didn't take a genius to see that Irene Roberts had feared the worst, and even knowing that David could still be alive couldn't entirely alleviate all of her past fears.

* * *

Tim Clancy offered T.J. coffee. T.J. declined. "This isn't a social visit, Mr. Clancy. I came about David Sinclair."

"I guessed that, but I told you all I know."

"Did you? What exactly did you do for the CIA, Mr. Clancy?"

"Paperwork, mostly. And occasionally I was sent out into the field."

"What if I said you were lying?"

"I'd say prove it." He smiled and lit his pipe. He looked like any ordinary retiree, and if T.J. hadn't known better, she'd have been taken in by him. The information that Pearl, bless her bureaucratic background, had found out, was making the difference between blind acceptance of his proclaimed position in the CIA, and the position T.J. had reason to suspect he'd really held.

She switched tactics for the moment. "Just how badly does the agency want David Sinclair?"

He drew on his pipe. The aromatic scent of it filled the air. "I'm sure they'd like to put the mystery of his disappearance to rest. They don't like loose ends. They'd like to know what happened to him."

"I think they'd like him dead, Mr. Clancy."

"Call me, Tim."

"It's true, isn't it?" T.J. said. "He wasn't a soldier of fortune, was he? He was CIA trained from the start. Trained by you. The rest of it, his being a secrets broker and jewel thief, was bogus information fed into CIA computers for people like Pearl to pick up. And you were no desk clerk or erstwhile agent. You were a CIA recruiter, your specialty recruiting potential assassins and double agents."

He didn't even blink. "Are you sure you won't have some coffee? It's really quite good. I make it from a special Colombian blend."

She ignored his hospitality, recognizing it for what it was a stall. "Did the agency send out scouts looking to liberate orphan boys from foster homes and into something far worse? Were you one of those liberators? The week that David ran away, two other boys ran off, too. By coincidence, both of the boys had lost their parents, just like David. One was living with an aged aunt; the other was also a foster child. They would have been ripe for adventure, a chance to be something other than a stranger in someone else's home."

"You're guessing, Miss McCall."

"Maybe. Tell me I'm wrong."

"You're very intelligent, and far too pretty to do what you do. You should be home raising children, or practicing law somewhere."

"So you checked into my background, too. You were expecting me to come back here?"

"I knew it was a possibility. Especially if you were as tenacious as Marshall says you are."

Marshall had brought her here to Clancy. How much did he know about the man facing her across the room? "Does Marsh know what you did for the CIA?"

"Marshall believes that I am what I purport myself to be, Miss McCall. Anything else is conjecture on your part."

"And if I said I could prove differently?"

He smiled. "But you can't. I know about your secretary. I know her sources, and I know their limitations. When you work for an intelligence agency, there are always rumors about what you do, or might be doing. It's the nature of the business. You get used to it."

"All right, then let me think out loud. You don't have to say anything if you don't want to, but feel free to jump in anytime you feel like it. For the sake of argument, let's say I'm right. Let's assume that David was pulled off the streets into the company. Let's assume he was trained to be an assassin or something just as valuable to the agency. Let's say that one day he began to go through burn-out, and he wanted to quit. That would have been catastrophic, wouldn't it? Especially if he insisted on leaving on his terms, not the agency's. Being the resourceful entity that it is, the agency might have used Michael to lure his brother into a trap. By now David would have known his only chance of surviving was to disappear. Let's say Michael found him, but wasn't able to hold him, and you lost David again. And let's say that you've been looking for him ever since."

He tapped his pipe on the corner of his ashtray. "I'm not looking for anyone, Miss McCall, I'm retired."

"A figure of speech. I mean the agency, of course."

He clapped his hands together and applauded her. "A very colorful and imaginative scenario, but that's all it is. If I'm to pretend you're right, then why would David expose himself after all this time by involving himself with someone as newsworthy as Joanne Kirkland?"

"Would you buy hiding in plain sight?"

"No, because David is too smart for that. It's the first place we ever look, and the last place anyone thinks we look. If David thought we were out to harm him, he wouldn't have been that careless. So, you see, David had, nor has, reason to fear the agency."

T.J. looked thoughtful. Her theory had sounded good when she'd tried it out on Gregg and Pearl, and she still believed in it. Yet Tim Clancy had a point. It was interesting, maybe even significant, that though he hadn't rubber stamped her theory, he hadn't vehemently denied it. "I think I'll have that coffee now," she said.

Thirty minutes later he walked her to the door. He reached out to shake her hand. "Be careful, Miss McCall. Be very careful."

There was more than concern in his voice. There was a clear cut warning. When she looked into his eyes she saw the truth mirrored there. Her theory about David, on or off the mark, had a trace of reality to it. That was what Tim Clancy's warning was intended to imply.

Chapter Seventeen

Hayward was proving he wasn't without influence, even this far from New York. Joanne had been indicted for Michael's murder, and Hayward was pushing for, and it looked like he was going to secure a speedy trial date. His explanation, when T.J. questioned the risks of forcing an early trial was typical of him, and by now not unexpected.

He said, in his own inimical way, "Joanne can't stand a long bout of negative publicity. I know those blood-thirsty press vultures," he growled. "Every day that passes is one more nail in her coffin."

"Don't you want to know what I'm doing to find David?" She asked.

He'd given her a strange look, one she couldn't decipher before he finally said," I just assumed you were doing your job. Neither Joanne, nor I, need details, Miss McCall, only results."

He'd dismissed her without as much as a backward glance.

* * *

Joanne looked calm and rested in the rustic setting of her living room. For a moment T.J. almost resented her tranquility. Everyone connected with the case was either working at a frenzy to insure her acquittal, or, like Hayward, they were noticeably concerned. Then she remembered how quickly she'd condemned Joanne once before, and was immediately conciliatory and tolerant.

T.J. accepted the glass of white wine Joanne offered. "You seem to be taking all this in stride, Joanne. Have you heard from David again?"

"No, but he'll come back. When all this is over, he'll come back to me."

T.J. set her glass down on the table before her. "When this is over, Joanne, you'll either be proven guilty, or someone else will be blamed for Michael's murder. That someone could be David. You said yourself..."

"That David killed Michael? It's true. David killed Michael to keep our love alive, but they'll never prove it." She gave T.J. an almost triumphant look. "And neither will you."

"You act like I'm the enemy. With that kind of attitude, you could spend the rest of your life in prison, Joanne."

Joanne shook her head. "Mr. Westfield is a brilliant attorney. Charlie said so. He'll get me off." She tipped her head to one side, staring at T.J. "Were you really married to Mr. Westfield?"

Impatience took over. "Yes, I was married to him, but that's beside the point, and yes, he is brilliant at what he does, I never denied that. But you're in one hell of a spot, if you don't take the stand and tell the jury what you told me about David killing his own brother."

"I won't do it. I'll say I don't remember what happened that night. I'll say I blacked out."

"How convenient. Just like you claim not to remember what happened at the boarding school. I know what happened there, Joanne. I talked to your former roommate. She told me all about your crush on Hawkins, and your self-abuse that night."

Joanne abruptly stood, waving her hands in the air angrily. "She's a liar. Hawkins was a janitor for God's sake! And I didn't abuse myself! Why would I do a thing like that?"

"Revenge and the need for attention, maybe both. Ann Sherwood is a nun, now. She has been for a long time. I don't think she was lying about what she saw that night, and her interpretation of what she saw seems genuine, not malicious."

"I don't remember anything that happened. If Ann really knows something why hasn't she said anything before now?"

"For the same reason that you never have, I suspect. Like you, she'd like to forget that night."

Joanne's face took on a faraway look, one that T.J. was beginning to recognize for an effective wall against facing the truth. She threw up her hands. "Have it your way. Your trial starts the day after tomorrow, and we're no closer to finding David Sinclair than the first day I met you. Do you know where he is? And, if you did, would you tell me?"

Her eyes, though still glazed, gave off a brief spark of life. "Don't be ridiculous. I'm the one who hired you to find him. Now, leave me alone and go do what you were hired to do."

* * *

T.J. had only seen Jim in action in court only once before, at Cryden's trial. That had been enough for her. It had been the beginning of the end for them, the last straw for an already embittered wife sickened by his adultery. Watching him now, she acknowledged that he really was as brilliant as he was reputed to be. Joanne was seated beside him, an annoying look of tranquility on her face. She was dressed conservatively in a dark blue suit with a plain white blouse, no make-up, except for a pale lipstick. She looked vulnerable. T.J. knew in her heart that Jim was responsible for both her choice of attire and her staged waif-like appearance. She looked innocent.

Yes, Jim was brilliant all right. And, ruthless. And, calculating. And...And what? T.J. forced herself to concentrate on the courtroom drama.

After the gun found in Joanne's toilet was identified as the murder weapon, the next witness for the prosecution was the police officer who'd found the gun.

Jim cross-examined from the defense table, his tone deceptively mild. "How did the defendant react to your finding the gun in her toilet?"

The prosecutor objected. "Calling for a conclusion from the witness, Your Honor."

Jim smiled over at the judge, Garth Hanson. Hanson was a man in his early sixties, acid tongued when he had to be, mildly firm when he wanted to be. "Your Honor," Jim said, "Since all the evidence against my client is circumstantial; I have to establish her mood the day she was arrested."

The judge allowed the question. Jim repeated it.

"She acted kind of funny," the policeman said. "She just smiled."

"Then she wasn't noticeably upset?"

"No."

"Thank, you. That's all," Jim said.

The fingerprint on the front door was introduced next, and established as belonging to Michael Sinclair. The prosecution stressed this phase of their evidence to establish Michael's presence at the house.

Jim addressed the forensic expert. "One print? Is that right?"

"Yes."

"No other prints inside the house indicating that Michael Sinclair ever went inside?"

"None that the crime lab people found."

"Thank, you."

Marshall was next to be called to the stand.

"You didn't find it strange that the only print belonging to the deceased was outside the house," Jim asked him.

"Not really. The inside of the house could have been wiped clean."

"So it could. But it could also mean that Michael Sinclair, who had been menacing his wife with strange phone calls for months, was trying to intimidate her further by lurking around the grounds of her house."

"We have only her word for it that there were any such phone calls."

"And we only have your assumption that Michael Sinclair was ever inside the house." Jim smiled triumphantly at the jury. "That's all for now, Detective."

The delivery boy was next. He was easy pickings for Jim. He brutalized the delivery boy in such a way that the twelve members of the jury were looking at the young man with pity, while still looking kindly on the man who'd delivered lethal blows in such a way that he seemed almost benevolent about it. Even as the boy left the stand, Jim shook his head sympathetically, as if to say that even the best-intentioned people made honest mistakes.

T.J. looked over at Marshall. Even though he'd expected no less from Jim, he was quietly angry. His case against Joanne had suffered the second of what he expected to be further paralyzing blows. The first, being his own brief cross-examination.

The judge called a recess until the next day. Hayward rose immediately and led Joanne out through the horde of reporters. T.J. made her own way out of the courtroom. She was almost to the open double doors when Jim called out to her. "A minute of your time, T.J.?"

T.J. had managed to avoid him since that night at her office. She knew it was unrealistic to think she could keep him at bay forever. "One minute. I have to get back to my office."

He slammed his briefcase shut and was quickly by her side. "Let's go out the side door. Hayward can beat off the press without me."

"All right."

"Follow me," he said. "Judge Lewis is out of town. We can use her chambers."

There had been rumors about Judge Marian Lewis and Jim Westfield. Only now it looked like there was truth to the rumors. Fifteen years his senior, some people claimed that he was climbing his way up through her bedroom. It bothered T.J. that she seemed to care. She chose belligerence and sarcasm as defense. "Then you are sleeping your way to the top.'

"You've been listening to jealous competitors. I said the room was available. But then so are others. If you'd prefer, we can go into one of them."

"No. Judge Lewis's chambers will be fine. Why would I care where we talk?"

"Another question you should be asking yourself."

Before she could respond, he guided her though a door marked JUDGE MARIAN LEWIS. He slid easily into her high-backed chair. "How does it look?"

"Like you were measuring yourself for it." T.J. looked down at her watch. "A minute you said. Your time is running out."

He leaned back in the chair, caressing the soft leather. "You haven't been telling me everything."

"I didn't know I was supposed to. I thought I was working for Joanne."

He jerked forward. "I'm her lawyer, damn it. Have you got a line on David yet?"

"Nothing concrete. Just a few theories."

"You want to share them?"

"Joanne still claims that David killed Michael. Do you plan to use that as a defense?"

"Strangely enough she never shared that piece of information with me, only with you. Do you know where Sinclair is?"

"Not yet. David worked for the CIA. He'd be good at hiding out."

Jim placed his fingers together. "I guess I'll have to bring up the fact that the Cadillac he supposedly left in, was found hidden on the grounds of her house. The police and the prosecution are trying to avoid bringing up that fact. They're saving it so that when Joanne beats this murder charge, they can put her on trial for the death of David Sinclair."

It was interesting, but not too surprising that Jim spoke in the positive vernacular. He didn't expect to lose this case. "Isn't that dangerous? It establishes the possibility that David is dead, murdered."

"It is dangerous, but then so is conviction. Find David Sinclair, T.J. If he didn't kill his brother he might know who did."

"What if it was Joanne herself?"

"Let me worry about that. Just find him."

"Don't think I don't want to." She said through gritted teeth. "He may have killed Scott."

* * *

Gregg was animated. "Our first real lead," he told T.J. "A guy answering David Sinclair's description was rushed to an emergency hospital in Montreal. It could track. Didn't he disappear from Canada?"

"Yes. I'll go there myself."

"I don't think that's smart, T.J. You're too close to this damn case. You're not being objective, anymore. I think you should stay here and keep an eye on Joanne, and on the trial. Don't you have to testify anyway?"

She frowned. Jim was calling her as a witness for the defense. She thought about their conversation when he'd brought the subject up.

He'd said, "I'm going to call you to the stand, T.J. You, more than anyone, except maybe Hayward, know just how fragile Joanne's hold on reality can be."

She'd bristled. "Then call Hayward."

"I will, but he'll be a somewhat hostile witness. He doesn't want me to focus on Joanne's mental state. Though God knows why."

Maybe it was her sense of fair play, or maybe T.J. just wanted to tell Jim something he didn't know, and should have. "You knew she was committed for three years."

"Sure. But she was never judged insane, just unstable. She says she was raped at that fancy boarding school her parents sent her to."

It was T.J. who was surprised. Joanne normally avoided saying anything about the incident at the school, using amnesia as a weapon against discussing it. "She wasn't raped, Jim." She gave him Sister Theodora's name and address. "Talk to her. She'll tell you what really happened at the school."

His eyes narrowed. "Why don't you tell me?"

Now she could get her own back. "All right. Sister Theodora used to be Ann Sherwood, Joanne's roommate at the school. She swears that Joanne committed self-abuse to discredit the janitor who spurned her advances. The headmistress talked to Joanne's parents the day after they took her away. They said she wasn't molested."

He looked at first disbelieving, then angry. "Of course they would say that. They wouldn't have wanted a scandal."

"Talk to the nun, Jim. I think you'll come away convinced."

"Why the hell didn't you tell me this before?"

"Because you never asked."

"What else are you keeping from me?"

She ignored his question. "Do you still want me to testify?"

"Damn you! Yes, I want you to testify, but if you have any more surprises up your sleeve you'd better lay them on me now. I don't think you hate me enough to want to burn Joanne to prove it."

"I don't hate...You're right. I wouldn't use another human being to get even."

His voice was hard. "You got even, T.J. You left me."

"Did you hear me?" Gregg's voice brought her back to the present.

"Yes, I heard you. Of course you have to go. Call me the moment you get to the hospital and you've seen the man they brought in? What was he brought in for, by the way?"

"Car wreck. Head injuries. He's unconscious."

"Then get going. I'll be waiting to hear from you."

* * *

T.J. decided it was time, that however slim the chances that the man in Montreal was David Sinclair, Joanne could stand to hear something hopeful.

Joanne didn't look like a woman under the threat of life imprisonment for murder, or worse, and once again, T.J. was struck by her apparent calm.

She invited T.J. in, served her wine, and then settled back to hear what T.J. had to say.

"We have a lead," T.J. said. "A slim one, and probably a false hope, but there's an accident victim in Montreal who might be David."

Joanne tensed up. "Really? When will you know?"

"Gregg is on his way up there now. I hope to hear from him by tomorrow, that is if they let him see the man and he can garner any useful information." T.J. shook her head. "I don't get it, Joanne. You should be jumping up and down with anticipation."

Joanne remained silent.

"Oh, I get it. You're afraid that if he's found he'll be charged with his brother's murder. You always knew that was a possibility. Unless, of course, you lied about who killed Michael. Did Hayward kill Michael?"

"Charlie was on the East Coast when Michael was killed."

"No, he wasn't. Pearl found out that he had his jet flown to an airport near here, the day Michael was killed."

"I didn't know!"

T.J. believed her. "It's a fact. We weren't able to get flight details until yesterday. His pilot was less than cooperative. When the jet left New York a flight plan was filed for Denver. Plans to land here were charted in mid-air. It must have been important for Hayward to want to come here, and use evasive tactics'. Did you see him?"

"No! I told you. I didn't even know he was here."

"Let's say I believe you. Is it possible he killed Michael? Think carefully before you answer."

Joanne seemed to weigh the choice ahead. A beloved husband or a trusted and valued father-like figure. The sacrificial lamb, when it came, surprised T.J. "No. David killed Michael. How many times do I have to tell you that?"

"Until I believe it, I guess. I have to tell Jim what I know about Hayward. I owe him that, and so do you."

"Of, course. But it won't make any difference."

Oddly enough, T.J. believed that Joanne believed the statement.

* * *

T.J. set the alarm for 6AM. Hopefully, Gregg would call her early. She fell into a restless sleep with images of Scott and Jim trying to pull her out of a fiery blaze. The night air was humid, and twice she kicked the covers aside.

In the middle of the night, T.J. stirred fitfully to escape her nightmares. She was wet with her own perspiration. She heard herself scream, so loud, and so real, that light sleeper that she was, she didn't hear the sound of the footstep in the hallway that led to her bedroom, nor was she aware of the doorknob slowly turning. Then, a sixth sense took over as a sliver of light illuminated the room from the lamp in the hallway that she left on nightly. It was a new habit, one acquired since Scott's death, one she saw as a weakness. The need for that kind of security would pass, she'd told herself.

T.J. shot up in bed, groggy from sleep, but with every nerve ending on full alert. She sensed, rather than saw the gun before it exploded in a flash of white light. She rolled to one side, feeling the bullet graze her side.

There was a flurry of footsteps and the sound of feet running down the hall to the elevators. T.J. was on her feet in seconds, ignoring her flimsy night attire as she ran barefooted down the hall only to see the elevator door close.

The stairs!

T.J. ran the five floors to the basement garage, the cold concrete lashing at her feet. By the time she arrived at the garage level, all that was left to see was the receding rear lights of a car speeding away.

Breathless, she glanced down at her leg. Blood was running in a steady stream from the graze inflicted by the assailant's bullet.

Angry at herself for not being more vigilant, she smashed her fist into the garage wall.

Once again someone thought she was closer to a solution to this case and Michael's murder than she really was. With a difference. This third attempt on her life was risky, desperate, and it was careless.

T.J. shivered uncontrollably. There would be no more sleep for her tonight.

Chapter Eighteen

T.J. pounded on the door of the high-rise luxury apartment. Getting here had been painful, both physically and emotionally. Yet, when she'd needed someone to talk to in the middle of the night, coming here seemed like the only logical place for her to be.

She'd hurriedly slipped into Levis and a shirt, both of which were now stained with her own blood. Exhausted from the night's events, the drive over here, and the effort to arouse the occupant of the apartment, she leaned against the door, clutching at her side.

After what seemed like an eternity, the door to the apartment swung open. Jim, his hair tousled, a robe tied sloppily around his waist, stared at her twisted form. "What the hell...?" He saw the blood soaked shirt and abruptly lifted her easily off the floor and took her inside. "My, God! What happened?"

Her voice was uneven, shaking. "I could use a drink."

He gently set her down on the couch, ignoring her protests as blood marred the fabric. "It'll clean. If it doesn't, I'll throw it out."

He came back a few seconds later with a glass filled with amber liquid. He lifted her head and placed the glass to her lips. "What happened?"

"Someone took a shot at me."

" What the hell are we into, T.J.?"

She appreciated the 'we.' "I don't know."

"Stay quiet," he cautioned. "Take off your clothes and let me see how bad it is."

They'd been married once, had seen each other naked a hundred times, and yet now she was shy about disrobing in front of him. "It's not that bad. The bullet barely grazed me. It's just a flesh wound."

"At least take off your shirt."

Her fingers shook as she began to work the buttons. Impatient, he helped her, and slipped the blouse from her shoulders and arms. His eyes lingered briefly on full breasts spilling from her white lace bra, then down to the wound itself.

"It's bad enough," he said. He undid the button on her Levis and pulled the zipper down a notch so he could see the rest of the wound. "I'll call a doctor."

"No! Don't! All it needs is some antiseptic. Do you have any?"

"Of course I do. Are you sure you don't want to see a doctor?"

"Perfectly sure."

He returned a few moments later with a bowl of water, a bottle of peroxide, gauze, and bandages. He carefully cleansed the area, and then he wet a piece of gauze with the peroxide. "This is going to hurt."

It did. When he had the wound bandaged he positioned himself on the corner of the couch facing her. "Did you see who it was?"

"No, I was asleep. I was having a nightmare. I have a lot of them since Scott died. Mostly, they're about him."

"And, tonight?"

"Yes." She wasn't going to tell Jim he'd played a part in tonight's nightmare. "Light entered the room. It woke me. Then there was the shot. I rolled away from it.' She shuddered. "If I hadn't, I'd be dead."

"And you saw no one?"

"No, just the glint of steel before the shot rang out. By the time I reached the hall, the elevator doors were closing. I took the stairs, but whoever it was had gotten away."

Jim paced the floor. "I'd like to kill the son of a bitch." He whirled around. "You have to stay here until this thing is over."

"Here! I can't stay here!"

"Why, not? It's the best possible place for you to be, and the last place anyone would expect you to be. Think about it."

"I can't stay here."

"Yes, you can. I have two bedrooms, and I won't attack you, if that's what you're worried about. I might still want you, but I would never force myself on you."

She flushed. He'd sensed her fear, but not the root of it. She was more afraid of her own feelings than his lust. "All right, I'll stay...and thanks."

"I should be thanking you. You were in trouble tonight, and you came here. It means that in spite of everything that's happened between us, you trust me. That means a lot."

"I had no where else to go," she said. "Marsh would have made me report the attempt on my life, and Pearl and Gregg would have told Marsh about it. In light of that, you were the only one I could turn to."

He made a face. "You still have the power to hurt me, T.J., even if it's only with words. Come on, I'll help you into bed. We'll get your things from the apartment in the morning."

Much later, unable to sleep, she couldn't block out the crushed look on Jim's face. She'd been cruel, and it wasn't justified. More importantly, and he must never know it, her actions were a defense against concern she might reveal her inner turmoil. She didn't hate Jim. She never had, and what she was feeling for him now, tonight, scared the hell out of her.

* * *

T.J. had finally fallen into a fitful sleep. She was awakened by the smell of frying bacon. She showered in the bathroom adjoining her bedroom, and when she came into the kitchen, a plate of bacon, eggs, hash browns, toast, with juice and coffee were waiting for her.

She started to say she didn't eat breakfast, but realized that Jim knew better. "You cooked all this?" she said.

"Yeah, I did. Try it. It's even edible. I've become a passably good cook. Living alone does that to you."

She ignored the jab. "What time is it?"

147

"There's time. Eat up and then we'll go get a few of your things. You can unpack while I'm in court."

She placed scrambled eggs on her fork. " I have to go to the office to see if Gregg's called, and then I'll come over to the courthouse." She wiped her mouth with the linen napkin by her plate. "Maybe I should just stay at my place. Whoever took a shot at me probably won't try it again."

"Not a chance. If you start to argue, I'll tell Marshall about the attempt on your life." He frowned. "You really should tell him anyway, T.J." And as she started to protest, "Forget I mentioned it. How's your side?"

"Sore, but I'll live. And please don't tell Marsh. He'll try to pull me off the case again."

"The man cares about you. So do I. Besides, there's evidence at your place. The bullet that grazed you is in there somewhere. It will tell us what kind of gun was used."

T.J. shook her head. "Not now. Maybe after I've had time to think it over."

"But you will think about it?"

"I promise."

"Who do you think was at the other end of the gun, T.J.?"

She'd thought about little else. "There are a few possibilities. David, if he's still in these parts. Hayward, but for the life of me I can't figure out why he'd want me dead, and the shadowy image of a perfect stranger."

"A stranger?"

"I've been thinking, Jim, what if someone who was looking for David Sinclair was watching Joanne's house, mistook Michael for David, and killed him by mistake."

"Like who?"

'I think David Sinclair knows too much. I think the CIA wants him dead."

"An interesting theory. If it's true, and if your scenario is correct, then why would Joanne say that David killed Michael?"

"A good question. A damn good question. I admit it doesn't make sense, unless..."

"Yes?" he prompted.

"Unless she didn't see anything that night, but just thinks it was David who killed Michael. She has blackouts, you know."

He frowned. "No, I didn't. Frequent?"

"You'd have to ask Hayward. I've never seen any myself, although I've seen her go into a trance-like state every once in a while. I think it's her way of escaping unpleasantness."

Jim reached over her to retrieve her plate. "You didn't eat much," he accused.

"It was good. I'm just not hungry."

He stared at her, his eyes saying more than words ever could. She suddenly felt uncomfortably warm. This scene was far too domestic and civilized. She liked it better when they were at war with each other.

She stood, the movement decisive. "Well, let's get going before you're late for court."

* * *

T.J. had barely entered her private office when Pearl buzzed her. "It's Gregg."

T.J. reached for the phone. The gesture hurt. Even though it was only a graze her side would be sore for days. "Gregg, did you talk to our mystery man?"

"No, he's still unconscious, but he's not David Sinclair."

"Are you sure?"

"I wasn't. Then a woman showed up who turned out to be the guy's girlfriend."

"What about I.D."

"It checks. He and the girl have been together off and on for ten years."

"Off and on?"

"I know what you're thinking, T.J., and it would have been nice, but there's no way its gong to track. This is not our boy. I called you earlier at your apartment, you didn't answer. Where were you?"

"I didn't hear the phone," she lied. "I must have been in the shower. Come on back, Gregg."

"I thought I'd poke around a bit in Quebec. Wasn't that where Sinclair supposedly disappeared from under the name of Jerry Crandall?"

"Yes, but the CIA must have lifted every rock more than once. I think you're wasting your time."

"Why don't I give it a shot anyway? What else do we have? Besides, they missed finding him with Joanne, so they're not perfect."

But they were resourceful. She thought about her slim escape from death last night, and her suspicions that they might be behind it somehow. "Okay, but be careful."

She checked her watch. The morning court session was underway. Jim was safely out of her hair and occupied.

T.J. grabbed her purse. As she passed Pearl's desk she said, "I have an errand to run, then I'll be in court. You can reach me there if you need me."

Fifteen minutes later she was back at her apartment looking for the bullet that had been meant to kill her, and missed.

* * *

T.J. found the bullet embedded in the mattress of her bed. She dug it out with a knife, staring at the scrap of metal that could have been her death warrant.

It had come from a .22 caliber gun. The same kind of gun that had killed Michael Sinclair. The same kind of gun David had given to Joanne. The same kind of gun carried by a professional.

T.J. emptied a bottle of aspirin and placed the bullet inside, then left the apartment. Staying with Jim might not be the best place, or the smartest place to be, but it was better than staying here.

* * *

T.J. slipped into the courtroom. The prosecution was just resting its case. The judge slammed his gavel down and called a recess until afternoon.

Jim turned to face her and came toward her. "Are you okay?"

"I'm fine. How'd it go?"

"Standard. They have a weak case. It's all circumstantial, but the jury might buy it if they see Joanne as a spoiled little rich girl, and not a frail human being. They have to start seeing her as a victim. I start my defense this afternoon. I'll get the preliminary examinations out of the way, and go for the gusto tomorrow. Hayward is right about one thing, the press is having a field day with this one. They haven't been kind to Joanne. I'll need you tomorrow. Are you ready to testify?

"If I have to. What is it you think I can say that will help your case?"

"Just answer my questions. Let me worry about the rest."

The thought of being subjected to questioning from the prosecution, wasn't nearly as disturbing as being put to the test by Jim. He'd proven time and time again that he was capable of sacrificing anyone to save his client.

Now it was her turn at the sacrificial altar.

* * *

It still felt strange to be in Jim's apartment, a guest, and yet more than a guest.

He insisted on making dinner, though she helped. He barbequed steaks, put potatoes in the microwave, and she tossed a salad and set the table.

To avoid any semblance of intimacy, T.J. steered the conversation in the direction of Joanne. "How's she holding up?"

"Better than I could have hoped for. But I've been watching the jury. They don't seem particularly disposed to like her." He shrugged. "I'll have to work on that."

She had sudden insight. "You think I can help you, don't you? Just exactly what kind of questions are you going to ask me?"

"Best you don't know up front, that way you'll be more natural. "He paused, took a sip of his wine, and said. "Don't mistake the way I treat you in court tomorrow with the way I feel about you outside the courtroom. I'll just be doing my job."

He was telling her that he wouldn't pull his punches. Then had she really expected him to? The kind of man he was in a courtroom had been partially to blame for their break-up in the first place.

T.J. downed the rest of her own wine. "Thanks for the warning, but I didn't need one. I have no illusions about tomorrow."

"And no illusions about me either?"

"None." She patted her lips with her napkin. "If I was a better person I'd offer to help you with the dishes, but I'm bushed, and my side hurts. I think I'll turn in early."

His hand lingered on her arm. "What are you afraid of, T.J.? Are you afraid to let yourself feel anything?"

"Not at all. I still feel love for Scott. His being gone doesn't change that." She made her way out of the room, turned at the doorway to the kitchen, and said, "Don't mistake my need for security for the way you want me to feel about you. We're history, Jim, and when this trial is over, and I've found David Sinclair, dead or alive, I don't expect that we'll be seeing each other again."

He filled his glass with the last of the wine. "I'll worry about that when the time comes. Sleep well."

For the most dangerous of moments she was tempted to go back to the table, but quickly left the room, thinking as she did, that if fear had wings, she was soaring.

Chapter Nineteen

Jim's opening statement was as always, convincing, and a trifle dramatic. He'd made a good stab at making Joanne out to be not only a victim of a husband who'd feigned his own death, but too delicate to commit premeditated murder.

T.J. was Jim's first important witness. She took the stand and was given the oath. She wore a conservative black pin striped pant suit, a silk blouse with a flattering bow, and pumps with medium-sized heels. She crossed her legs and clasped her hands together, waiting for Jim to start his examination.

Her hands were clammy. She felt beads of sweat gathering beneath her auburn bangs. She looked over at Joanne. It was the only time since the case against her had begun that Joanne had looked noticeably perturbed.

It's me, T.J. thought. She's worried about what I might say. T.J. tried to give Joanne a reassuring smile, and found she couldn't, and was bothered by that. Joanne was, after all, her client.

Jim noted the brief exchange between the two women. He smiled for effect, but T.J. saw that he was tensing up. He too, was worried about what she might say, she acknowledged. For a brief moment she felt power over him and Joanne. Brief, because she knew the feeling was an illusionary and an unworthy one.

"Would you tell the court, Miss McCall, what your relationship is to the defendant, Joanne Sinclair?" Jim asked. There was no hint of warmth on his face. He was all business, all lawyer. As it should be, T.J. acknowledged. But that didn't mean she had to like the position she now found herself in.

"Joanne is my client."

"Would you tell the court what it was that you do for a living?"

"I'm a private investigator."

"And Joanne Sinclair hired you to do what for her?"

"She hired me to find her husband."

"The murder victim, Michael Sinclair?"

"No. she hired me to find David Sinclair."

"Her second husband?"

"Well, not exactly. Joanne and David Sinclair were never officially married."

"But you thought he was her husband when she hired you?'

"For a while, yes."

"Did you find him?"

"You know I didn't."

Jim smiled, but the expression didn't reach his eyes. "The court doesn't know that, Miss McCall."

T.J. flushed. "I never found David Sinclair. I'm still looking for him."

"What relation, if any, is David Sinclair to the dead man?"

"He's his brother."

Jim moved to the defendant's table and took a sip from a glass of water. He had established in the jury's mind that David Sinclair was alive with his use of the present tense. Again, T.J. glanced over at Joanne. She was definitely on edge.

"Did Joanne Sinclair ever mention the decedent to you?" Jim asked.

"Anything she and I discussed is privileged information."

"But you did find out that Joanne Sinclair had been married to Michael Sinclair, and that he was presumed dead, did you not?"

"Yes."

"Was Joanne Sinclair distraught when she came to you the day she hired you?"

T.J. hesitated. "Distraught is not exactly the right word."

"Then what is the right word?"

"She seemed lost."

Jim leaned closer to her. "Lost? That's an odd way of putting it. It was her husband who was missing. Excuse me, her lover. But she seemed lost? Is that what you're implying?"

"Yes. I mean...Well, she had...Yes, lost is the right word."

Jim paced the floor in front of her. He'd sensed that T.J. had started to say that Joanne had lied about her true identity.

The prosecutor stood. "I object, Your Honor, council is leading the witness and calling for a conclusion."

"On the contrary, Your Honor," Jim countered. "Miss McCall is an expert witness. In her line of work she constantly has to make judgment calls as to the mood of an individual." He smiled again. This time the smile reached his eyes. "That's what makes her tops in her field."

"I'll allow it, but please begin a new line of questioning," Judge Garth Hanson said.

"Think carefully before you answer this next question," Jim continued. "Did you at any time consider that your client, Joanne Sinclair, had reason to fear for her life?"

"I uh...No, I don't recall ever thinking that."

"Why, not? Your own life was threatened. Your car was run off the road, your house burned, and..."

Distress heightened the green in T.J.'s eyes. She looked past the others over to Marshall. He was leaning forward in his seat.

"It must have occurred to you," Jim insisted, "or it should have, that if someone wanted to harm you, your client could be next in the line of fire."

T.J. flushed angrily. "It never did."

"Why not?" Jim persisted.

The prosecutor stood again. "Objection, Your Honor, counsel is badgering his own witness."

"I'm inclined to agree with the prosecutor, Mr. Westfield. Is there a point to this line of questioning?" Judge Hanson asked.

"Yes, Your Honor, there is a point to be made. If you'll just allow the witness to answer my question, I'll prove it."

"All right. But get to the point quickly. Answer the question, Miss McCall."

"Would you please repeat the question," T.J. said.

"I asked you why it never occurred to you that your client, Joanne Sinclair, might also be in danger, and you said it hadn't occurred to you." He pushed himself forward, his hands resting on the witness stand. "Why were you so sure she was not in harm's way?"

"Because I had, have reason, to believe that attempts made on my own life might have been made by David Sinclair."

Jim looked triumphant. Not only had he established the possibility that David Sinclair was alive, he'd painted a picture of a man capable of murder. "And David Sinclair in your opinion would never harm the defendant. Is that correct?"

T.J. stared past him. "I'm not sure."

" I see. A moment ago, you were sure."

"Your Honor," the prosecutor objected, on his feet now. "Really! Counsel for the defense is going far afield from this case. David Sinclair is not on trial here. Joanne Sinclair is."

"Objection sustained. You were cautioned, Mr. Westfield. I can no longer indulge this line of questioning."

Jim turned away from T.J. and faced the jury. "That's all, Miss McCall. Thank you."

This time when T.J. looked over at Joanne, her usually emotionless face was filled with pure hatred.

*　*　*

The prosecutor, Wendell David, thirtyish, was an ambitious slightly obese individual who had begun his career as a defense attorney. To win this particular case would place him at the top of the heap in an office filled with ambitious prosecuting attorneys. T.J. could see the need to win in his facial expression, in his every body movement. Like Jim, he would spare nothing, or no one, to reach his goal.

"Miss McCall," he began, "Would it be fair to state that since Joanne Sinclair is your client, you're biased to say only favorable comments on her behalf?"

T.J. noted only slight malevolence now in Joanne's expression. "No, it wouldn't be fair to say that at all. I'm here to tell the truth."

"Whatever that may be." And at a warning glance from Judge Hanson, "Strike that last statement. Did you ever have reason to discuss Michael Sinclair with Mrs. Sinclair?"

"Discussions between me and my client are confidential. You, like the defense attorney already know that."

He smiled. "So we do. Did you ever meet Michael Sinclair?"

T.J. shot an angry glance over at Marshall, feeling betrayed. She'd confided in him, trusted him. "I may have."

"You may have?"

"Yes. A man followed me to London. At first I thought it might be David Sinclair. Later, I decided it was probably his brother Michael."

He produced a blow-up of the body found on shore. "Is this the man who you believed to be Michael Sinclair?"

T.J. took the photo from him. "The man I met had a beard and contact lenses. This man is clean shaven. I don't know if they were the same man or not. If pressed, I would have to say I've never met the man in this photograph."

"But they might have been one and the same?"

"It's possible, I suppose."

"You had reason to believe that Michael Sinclair, presumed dead, was really alive?"

"Yes."

"Did you tell your client that you thought it was possible that her husband was alive?"

"If I had, the answer would have to be that any conversation between my client and myself is confidential."

He began to swivel around to face the jury, a look of satisfaction of his face, when T.J. added, " I never shared that information with

Joanne when I began to suspect he might still be alive, because I had no proof."

Triumph was replaced by anger and frustration. "I see. That will be all, Miss McCall."

T.J. stepped down and when she passed Jim, he gave her a wink and a look of approval. She left the court room, made her way down the wide marble-floored staircase to the parking lot and sped off. She opened all the windows letting the wind whip through her hair. A half-hour later she parked at the beach, calm enough finally to deal with the events of the day.

She was haunted by omissions in her testimony. She hadn't outright lied on the stand, but she hadn't volunteered that Hayward had told her he'd sent Michael to London to follow her. Then again, was it her fault that the prosecutor hadn't asked the right questions?

She was getting too close to this court case because she was staying with Jim. That had to change. Tonight she decided, would be the last time she would stay at his apartment. Tomorrow, she would find another place to go even if it meant staying in a hotel.

* * *

Dinner was a difficult meal. Jim wanted to talk about the trial. T.J. didn't.

"I wasn't that rough on you," Jim said moments after they left the table. "Why are you so upset?"

"I didn't like you very much today. You were gloating. I wasn't too crazy about myself, either. I'll look for another place to stay tomorrow. In any case, I won't be staying here after tonight." She feigned a stretch. "I think I'll turn in now."

Jim grabbed her by the arm, restraining her, whirling her around to face him. He pulled her so close that she could feel his breath on her face. Then suddenly, and unexpectedly, he drew her to him and his lips crushed down on hers.

She fought to escape and pulled herself free. She stepped back and slapped him. Red welts appeared on his face.

He seized her wrist before she could strike him again. "That's the second time you've physically attacked me. Why? Admit it. You want me as much as I want you."

She jerked herself free. "I'd rather bed down with a snake."

She left him standing there, an angry look on his face. When she reached her room, she slammed the door shut and placed a chair under the doorknob. She was shaking so badly her teeth began to chatter. "You asked for it, she silently accused herself. You came here knowing this could happen. Maybe in some sick kind of way, you wanted it to happen."

She hugged her waist with her arms. Tears sprang to her eyes. "I'm sorry, Scott, she whispered. "Sometimes it's hard to even remember what you looked like. Why did you have to leave me?" She longed for the touch of a caring human being, wanted to be held, craving warmth. Scott had given all those things, and for a while, in the early years of their relationship, so had Jim.

Later, the apartment quiet except for the chimes of the grandfather clock in the hall, she tossed around, unable to sleep. Twice, she heard Jim leave his room and go into the kitchen. He was as restless as she was. Once, she thought she saw the doorknob to her room gently turning.

She buried her head in the pillow. She should leave now, in the middle of the night, be gone by the time he woke up. It would be better that way.

And it would solve nothing.

She slipped out of bed and padded barefoot out of the room, and entered the hall. Jim's room was a few feet away. She stood in front of his door, her heart pounding. She twisted the doorknob and eased the door open.

He was awake, lying on his back, his hands behind his head. She closed the door behind her, slid the straps of her gown off her shoulders and let it fall to the floor. Her nakedness was outlined by the soft glow of moonlight.

T.J. approached his bed. She could hear his labored breathing. His eyes followed her every move. He didn't seem surprised to see her, only expectant.

She slid into bed beside him. "Don't get the wrong idea," she said. "All this is...is sex."

Chapter Twenty

T.J., disgusted at herself for giving in to her need for raw sex, was gratified to see that Jim had left the apartment early when she awoke and made her way into the kitchen.

Afterward, she'd ended up in her own room. Ran there really, unable to face him. It hadn't helped to admit that last night had been good for her, but then sexual satisfaction had never been one of their problems. What had gotten into her? Jim wasn't Scott. On his best day he wasn't good enough to walk in Scott's shadow and now, she had betrayed even his memory.

She was on her way out of the apartment when the phone rang. She wasn't going to answer it but the ringing was insistent, urgent. She finally picked up the receiver. "Hello."

"T.J., it's me, Jim. How are you feeling this morning?"

"A little like a whore. Last night didn't mean anything, Jim. I'm sorry I let it happen."

"You made it happen, and I'm not one bit sorry. Now may not be the time, but you should know that I still..."

He was going to tell her he still loved her. T.J. swallowed. "You're right. It's not the time, nor will there ever be a right time. I won't be here when you come home. I'll stay in a hotel."

"That's not necessary."

"I think it is."

She was about to hang up when he said, "I called to tell you that I'm putting Joanne on the stand today. I don't think I have a better witness in this case than the woman herself. I know she's vulnerable and weak, and you know it, but I have to make the jury believe it. I thought you'd want to be here."

161

T.J. was torn. She had work to do, but she wanted to see how Joanne handled taking the stand.

"What does Hayward say about this?"

"He doesn't know. By the time he finds out it will be too late."

"What if putting her on the stand backfires on you?"

"I'll take my chances. If I don't put her on the stand, I think the best we can hope for is a hung jury. She can't take another trial. If she reacts the way I think she will to questioning, she'll convince them she has problems with reality. Then I'll change the plea to diminished capacity."

"Hayward will have a fit."

"She's MY client. Anything more on the whereabouts of David Sinclair?"

"I was just about to leave for my office and get an update when you called. If there's anything significant, I'll let you know."

* * *

T.J. slipped into the courtroom. Joanne, dressed in a simple blue dress with a white Peter Pan collar was taking the oath. Hayward was not in court.

Jim smiled at Joanne encouragingly. "Do you understand the charges that have been brought against you, Mrs. Sinclair?"

"Yes, I do."

"Did you murder Michael Sinclair?"

Joanne cleared her throat. She looked around the room. A look that T.J. had begun to anticipate started to spread across her face. In a few seconds Joanne stared unseeingly back at Jim.

"Mrs. Sinclair, I asked you if you killed your husband."

There was a gradual recovery. T.J. glanced at the jury. They appeared mesmerized by Joanne's swiftly changing mood swings.

"What did you say?"

"Did you kill your husband?"

"David isn't dead."

"We're talking about Michael Sinclair, your first and only legal husband. Did you kill him, Joanne?"

"Joanne passed her hand across her brow. "I really don't feel very well. You see, I'm pregnant."

*　*　*

Pandemonium spread throughout the courtroom. Reporters rushed into the hall to use the phones. Jim wheeled around, and when his eyes met T.J.'s, the accusation that he was grandstanding she'd intended to hurl at him, never left her lips. Jim was as shocked by Joanne's statement as was everyone else in the courtroom.

T.J. left the room, pausing by the busy phones. She overheard one reporter saying, "What a bombshell! Joanne Sinclair just told the world that she's pregnant, which leaves the sixty-four thousand dollar question unanswered. Who the hell is the father? Supposedly, her live-in lover has been gone for months, and she claims she never saw Michael Sinclair more recently than nine years ago. You know what I think? I think Michael Sinclair wanted something from his wife, probably money, he fucked her, and then she saw through him and she killed him."

The headlines, which would likely read, WHO IS THE FATHER OF JOANNE SINCLAIR'S CHILD? was the burning question that T.J. wanted an answer to. How many times had she doubted Joanne's claim that David Sinclair had come back into Joanne's life, however briefly?

When she reached the parking lot she climbed into her car, and called her office on her cell phone. When Pearl answered, she said, "Get Gregg back here right away. I don't think David Sinclair is anywhere near Canada. I think he's within grabbing distance. Joanne may have just thrown out the bait that will reel him in."

*　*　*

163

T.J. was on the phone when Jim pushed his way into her office. "You have to believe I didn't know she was going to do that," he said. " What a mess! Half the press is building a case against her implying she slept with Michael Sinclair recently enough to bear his child, and the other half? Well, they don't know what we know, do they? They don't know that Joanne saw David Sinclair very recently. All they have is that he disappeared out of her life too long ago to be the biological father of her child." He slammed his fist down on her desk. "Damn her! She should have told me about this."

T.J. almost felt sorry for him. "I figure this will bring David Sinclair in, Jim. Can you buy me some time?"

"I'll try. Are you coming home tonight?"

"I thought I made it clear that I'm staying in a hotel."

"All you made clear, T.J., was that we needed what we had last night. I'm not going to mince words. I want you again."

T.J. looked up and saw Pearl hovering in the doorway. She paled. That's all she needed right now, Pearl jumping all over her case.

"It's not open for discussion, Jim."

He saw Pearl, too. "I'll be in touch."

Pearl looked at his departing figure. "You've been at his place?"

T.J. sighed. "Yes. Someone took a shot at me two nights ago. I was afraid to go back to my place, and I didn't want you, Marsh, or Gregg to know about it. Jim was convenient."

Pearl clucked. She shook her head. "You slept with him."

T.J. flushed angrily. "You're stepping over the line, Pearl. You're not my mother, and you're not my keeper. What I do with my personal life is just that, personal."

Pearl nodded. "Okay."

She was hurt. T.J. wanted to put her arms around her, but didn't. "Listen, this has been a tough case, but I think it's about over."

"Except someone may still wants you dead!"

"Then we just won't let that happen, will we?"

"I'm probably going to hate myself for this," Pearl said, "But maybe you should stay at Jim's. It's the last place anyone will look

for you. The last damned place I would have expected to find you."
She glared at T.J.

"That's why I went there in the first place. No, I'll stay in a hotel. I won't be easy to find, I promise. Not until we have the answer to who wants me dead, anyway.

* * *

Three hours later, Marshall called her. "Thought you'd like to know. Joanne Sinclair is off the hook. Judge will probably dismiss the case against her tomorrow morning." He paused. "Someone else confessed to killing Michael Sinclair."

"David?"

"No. As far as I know Sinclair is still missing, maybe dead."

"Then, who?"

"Charlton Hayward. We booked him an hour ago."

* * *

Joanne was seeing no one. Hayward, due out on bail in the morning, was still behind bars. T.J. talked Marshall into letting her see him.

It wasn't right, T.J. couldn't help thinking. The image of a man of Hayward's stature incarcerated for murder was too bizarre. Yet, except for the pain that filled his eyes, he didn't seem unduly upset at receiving T.J. in these sordid surroundings.

"You killed him?" T.J. said.

"Why are you so surprised? Isn't it what you always suspected?"

"There were moments, I admit that. I just can't bring myself to believe you really did it."

"You mean now that I've confessed? What's the matter, Miss McCall? Is my turning out to be the villain of the piece so hard to take?"

"Strangely enough, it is. You really killed him?"

"Yes, and I'm not sorry. I only have one regret, and that is that Joanne had to endure any of this, especially the trial." His eyes flashed angrily. "I told that ex-husband of yours that under no circumstances did I want Joanne to take the stand. When I heard what happened in court…"

"You weren't there that day. Where were you?"

He shrugged. "A small medical problem, nothing serious. I was in the emergency room."

"What kind of medical problem?"

"I think that's highly personal, Miss McCall, and not relevant to my confession."

"It might be if you had a terminal disease and decided to sacrifice your life so that Joanne might go free."

"That's very melodramatic, and it isn't true. I told you, the problem was a minor one. I'll live to serve out whatever sentence the court passes."

"Then answer me this. I always believed that whoever killed Michael Sinclair tried to kill me. Was it you who ran me off the road?" She clenched her fists. "And was it you who burned my home and killed my boyfriend? Did you take a shot at me the other night?"

He nodded. "Yes, and I am sorry about your friend." He looked genuinely sorry.

She knew what it felt like to want to kill, and to hell with the consequences. Only the glass partition that separated them stopped her from leaping at him. "Why? What did I know?"

"More than you were aware."

"To hell with you. What makes you tick, Hayward? You had the world on a string. You were one of the most respected attorneys in the country. You had everything. Why? In God's name, why? What was worth killing for, and ruining your life and those of others? You took something very precious from me. Scott was my lifeline. I loved him. Worse, you made me afraid of dying, because when Scott died I realized that I wasn't immortal. Strange, isn't it, but I used to think I was."

"I did what I did, for Joanne. I don't know how many times I tried to tell you how strongly I was motivated to do just that."

"I wish I had taken you more seriously. Joanne is your daughter. At least you think she is. I guess it's true what they say about blood being thicker than water."

He looked tired. "I think we can end this conversation now. You have what you came for."

"I haven't found David."

"You can stop looking. I killed him, too. He's buried where no one will ever find him."

* * *

It was late. Pearl had gone home hours ago. T.J. looked up when she heard the sound of footsteps. It was Gregg.

He plopped himself down in a chair. "I just got in. I heard the news. What now, T.J.?"

"I went to see Hayward. He confessed to everything. To killing Michael, to trying to kill me, to killing David Sinclair."

"David Sinclair is dead!"

She didn't answer.

"T.J.?"

She reached into the file lying on her desk, Joanne's file. She pulled out the photo of David that Joanne had given her. "Get someone to tell you how old this picture is. Can you have the information to me by tomorrow?"

"Sure. What gives? If he's dead..."

"A hunch, Gregg. Just a hunch. Humor me and go along with me on this."

"What will you be doing?"

"Seeing a doctor. Maybe, two."

* * *

167

The case against Joanne was dismissed early the next morning. Pearl called T.J. on her cell phone to tell her that Jim had phoned her three times.

"Do you want me to give him your mobile number?"

"No, Pearl. I'm not ready to talk to him yet. Its official then? Joanne is out of the woods?"

"As of an hour ago. Jim isn't wasting any time. He's representing Hayward now, and he's pushing for an early preliminary trial."

"Are you a betting lady, Pearl?"

"You know I never gamble. Just getting up in the morning at my age is gamble enough."

"Too, bad. If you were a gambler, I'd say it would be reasonably safe to say that there will be no trial."

"What have you got up your sleeve?"

"An end to this case if my hunch is right. Hopefully, I'll have some more answers later today. Call me when Gregg gets the information on the photo of David Sinclair I gave him."

"But the case is over...isn't it"

"Not necessarily so," T.J. responded.

Two hours after visiting two medical facilities, T.J.'s hunch was proving to be more than just a lucky guess, with one nasty little flaw. She still didn't know for sure who'd killed Michael Sinclair, or who'd terrorized and threatened her.

But now she could hazard one hell of a good guess now that she knew the motive.

Chapter Twenty-One

T.J. stepped back from the chalkboard she used, like some writers used a storyboard. On it she had written;

HAYWARD IS NOT DYING.
JOANNE IS NOT PREGNANT.
DAVID SINCLAIR HAS NO MOTIVE TO KILL HIS BROTHER.
NO PRINTS?
NO ONE EVER SAW DAVID.

She was surveying her handiwork when Gregg came in. He handed her the photo of David Sinclair. "My expert says that this photograph is about fifteen years old, taken from a distance, and with a not too sophisticated camera. Does any of that support your hunch?"

She fingered the snapshot. "Yes, it does." She turned back to the board and wrote:

PICTURE OF DAVID IS 15 YEARS OLD

"How'd you make out with the doctors?" Gregg asked.

"A blank, but I expected that." She wrinkled her nose. "Ethics always get in the way, you know that. But I did find out what I wanted to know by going through the back door."

"What were you looking for?"

"Missing pieces. I confirmed one of my suspicions, and I got a bonus I didn't expect. I was laboring under the mistaken impression that Hayward is terminally ill and he's sacrificing himself for

Joanne. It turns out that Hayward is suffering from nothing more serious than a painful, but treatable ulcer."

Gregg placed his feet on her desktop. "Which means what? That he's guilty?"

"Only of loving Joanne's mother, and then her daughter, and of sometimes confusing the two, I suspect."

"He didn't kill Michael Sinclair then?"

"No."

"How can you be so sure? He was here the night Michael Sinclair was killed. We've proven that."

"He has an alibi, one he didn't expect to surface this quickly."

"An alibi?"

T.J. moved from behind her desk. She gently slapped Gregg's feet to the floor. "That's mahogany, you moron. It's true, Hayward did fly here. Not long after his plane landed, his pilot, who also acted as his chauffer, turned back on the way to Joanne's house and took his boss to the emergency center. Just as Hayward had to be taken there the day Joanne testified in court. He has a reoccurring problem, one that Hayward hadn't taken time to have checked. On the night Michael Sinclair was killed, his pain was so excruciating, that his chauffer panicked. Hayward was treated, and was kept for overnight observation."

"How'd you find this out?"

"Sometimes you get lucky and find a talkative and cooperative nurse or receptionist." She grinned. "Take you and that blonde at the sanitarium where Joanne was kept, for instance. I got lucky. I found both a talkative nurse's aide, and a cooperative receptionist. I was, as I said, operating on the premise that Hayward had been given a death sentence. Instead, I found out that his admittance to emergency services the day Joanne testified was his second such admittance to the center. His chauffer filled in the rest of the gaps for me. He was very anxious to talk. He wants to see his boss freed from a murder charge. Nothing altruist, you understand. If Hayward is convicted of murder, he's out of a job."

"If Hayward didn't kill Michael, who did?" Gregg checked the board behind her. Not David you say? Then, who?"

"I think we can definitely rule out David." She looked over at the clock on the wall. "I have an appointment to see Tim Clancy. Want to come with me?"

He eased himself out of the chair. "Try to stop me. You can fill me in on why we're going to see him on the way over there." And at T.J.'s winsome look, "Ah, come on, T.J. Give a guy a break. You are going to fill me in?"

Her smile lit up her eyes, making them seem greener, more luminous. "Pearl says that I'm like a teenager on prom night when a case comes together. Right now I feel like one. Of course, I'll fill you in."

Tim Clancy gave Gregg a questioning look. "My associate, Gregg, Mr. Clancy," T.J. said as way of an introduction. "We've been working closely together to find David Sinclair."

"You think I know where he is?"

"If anyone does, you do. It took me a while, but the way I have it worked out is that you've been protecting him. You and he became close, didn't you? You helped him to escape the agency's clutches when he disappeared from Canada. I remember thinking that you were more than just surprised when you heard about him and Joanne. You were angry. You wondered why he'd left whatever carefully planned hideout you'd found for him to link up with a woman of Joanne's background. Why, you must have asked yourself, over and over again, did a man who had so much to lose by coming out of hiding, risk everything, including his life? For the love of a woman? This wasn't the David Sinclair you knew, was it? The David Sinclair of your memory would have never connected with someone like Joanne. It would have been like committing suicide."

Tim Clancy gave her a shrewd look. "The agency would do well to recruit you, Miss McCall. You think along the same lines. I saw that in you the first day you came here. You had all the pieces to the puzzle. All you had to do was make them fit. Do they fit now?"

She nodded. "They're beginning to."

"Then come with me," he said. "I have someone I think you should meet." When Gregg stepped forward with her, he added. "Just the lady. No offense."

T.J. nodded at Gregg. "Stay here. I'll be all right."

She followed Clancy out beyond his small house to a detached garage that had a small room abutting it. Clancy opened the door of the room with a key that he extracted from his cardigan pocket. He swung the door open.

It was still daylight, though dusk was imminent. There was no interior lighting on, or any light except the waning rays from a dying sun coming from a single window. Clancy ushered her inside. He pulled on a string hanging from a light bulb in the ceiling.

The room was occupied. "I'd like you to meet David Sinclair, Miss McCall," Clancy said. "I think it's time."

* * *

T.J. was the last to arrive at Joanne's house. Hayward, out on bail, and Jim and Gregg were already there by her invitation.

T.J. admitted that arriving late was dramatic a la Perry Mason, or the like, but she hadn't been able to resist the urge to be dramatic. It was a small concession to herself. She'd traveled a long hard road to get to this point, and people had been hurt, and Scott was dead. And all because a woman had reported her live-in lover missing. It should have been simple; it just hadn't turned out that way.

Jim, ever in charge, opened the door to her. "Well, you finally made it. What's this all about, T.J.?"

"Everyone's here?"

"As you ordered. You're the last, and the main attraction. They're all in the living room."

"Thanks. Could you get me a glass of wine, please?"

A few minutes later, a full glass in her hand, T.J. stood in the center of the living room studying the occupants of the room. Hayward looked pale, not surprising, considering his condition, and what he'd been through in the last twenty-four hours. It must have been humiliating for him to have endured fingerprinting, mug shots, and a strip search.

Gregg looked expectant, and slightly amused. He knew most of what was going to occur here. Besides T.J., he was the only one who did.

Jim, a highball by his side, looked interested, with a disturbingly sensual look in his eyes. He was thinking about the night he and T.J. had spent engaged in animal passion. His eyes told her he wanted her. T.J. looked away, and over at Joanne.

Joanne was ready, T.J. knew, to drift off into a dimension of her own making at any provocation, and T.J. was going to give her that provocation. Gregg, coached by T.J., was ready to spot the tell-tale signs of mental retreat and react to them.

"Good news, everyone," T.J. announced. "I've found David."

T.J. had thought she was ready for any eventuality, but a chill ran down her spine as a blood-curdling scream left Joanne's lips. The sound, which seemed never-ending, filled the room, and was so intense, that when Hayward dropped his half-full glass of Scotch to the floor and it shattered and no one seemed to notice.

*　*　*

The room was finally quiet. "Look what you've done!" Hayward accused. "You could have broken it to her gently, and privately," he added, his tone acid.

"So that she could continue to play head games with herself, and with me?" T.J. said. "Not a chance."

Jim, who until now had watched the melodrama without comment, said, "So where the hell is Sinclair, and where did you find him?"

"He found me, really."

"And?"

"We talked. It was very informative." She looked over at Joanne. "You should have made someone up who didn't exist, Joanne. But then you thought it was a safe fantasy, didn't you, because Michael told you David was dead. But then a lot of people thought he was dead. Clancy's doing. He was protecting David Sinclair."

"Do you mind telling me what the hell is going on?" Jim said.

"Parts of it I can only guess and parts of it David Sinclair supplied. You're the only one here, Jim, who doesn't know that David Sinclair, though he existed, never existed in Joanne's life."

"Come again," Jim said, a frown of incomprehension on his face.

"It's simple," T.J. said. "Joanne made him up."

"But you said you found him," Jim said. There was exasperation in his voice.

"I did. Sit down, Jim, and I'll walk you though it as best I can." Her eyes connected with Hayward. "None of this surprises you, does it? You knew all along that Joanne was having a delusory relationship with David Sinclair."

Hayward held Joanne close. She was off in another dimension, silently shaking, tears rolling down her cheeks. "You're telling the story. I, for one, would like to know what you think you've come up with."

"Playtime is over, Mr. Hayward. I'm not guessing. The truth was always there, hovering on the surface, so simple that I couldn't see it. You can't protect her any more, but you can help her. God knows someone needs to. Look at her. She needs the kind of help you can't give her, and there are worse places to be than a qualified institution. The incident at the English boarding school was a stepping off point for Joanne. She's lived on the edge of reality, on the edge of madness ever since. For a moment, when she met Michael Sinclair, she knew brief happiness, but then he turned out to be a user, worsening her mental state. He told Joanne about his brother. Michael hated his brother, and that was enough to make him a hero, a knight in shining armor in Joanne's eyes, so she invented his presence in her life. She made him into everything she'd ever dreamed or wanted a man to be."

"Wait a minute, T.J.," Jim interrupted. "How did she get away with that?"

"She had help. Mr. Hayward allowed her to keep her illusion alive. He even confessed to killing David to spare Joanne from the pathetic truth. He sent her here, to this place, a place so isolated; it wouldn't seem strange that no one ever met her new husband. Of course, there never was a marriage, that's why no record exists. Sloppy, Mr. Hayward. You should have had a John Doe from the streets stand up with her. Gregg talked to the Kirkland housekeeper. She told him that no one ever saw Joanne's new lover, and when she became too nosy, she was let go. That's when you sent Joanne here, wasn't it, Mr. Hayward? Then, one day, for whatever reason, her fantasy existence with David Sinclair went sour. Only she knows why."

Joanne stared ahead of her, saying nothing, but for a moment there was a glimmer of understanding in her eyes.

"Someday she may be able to tell us," T.J. went on. "I do know the fateful day, the day that changed all our lives, she did the unexpected. Usually, when she had a problem, she called her trusted friend and attorney, but this time, she took her fantasy to new extremes. She reported David Sinclair missing, and she hired me. That must have really given you heartburn, Mr. Hayward. What to do now? You could have told me the truth, and I think you tried to once, but that would have meant having her committed, and you couldn't make yourself do that. You should have, you know. You'll have to now. Difference is, that if you'd done it back then, two people needn't have died, which makes you an accomplice, Mr. Hayward, so you'll be needing a lawyer after all."

"Who the hell did kill Michael Sinclair?", Jim asked.

"Your original client. Joanne killed Michael. She killed him when he tracked her down. He was probably trying to blackmail her by threatening to blow the lid on her fantasy. Michael Sinclair believed David to be dead. The CIA had told him he was. Michael was a cruel man. Chances are he goaded Joanne into killing him by belittling her."

"He called me a fool."

175

Everyone stared at Joanne, back amongst them now. "He called me an ugly, lonely, pathetic fool. I told him about David. He laughed at me. He said that David wouldn't have given me a second look, so I killed him. It was the only way to get David to come back to me. And he did," she said triumphantly. "Now I'm going to have his child."

T.J. knew that Joanne's thread on reality could be lost in seconds. She pressed on. "It was you in the car the night I was ran off the road, wasn't it?"

"You were getting too close. I had to stop what I'd started. I didn't want you to find David anymore. I was afraid you'd scare him off."

"And the fire at my house?"

"You should have died then. It would have been over. Michael was so easy to kill. He never expected his mousy, timid little wife to shoot him. But you went on living. I saw your car burning, yet you survived!"

"You took a shot at me?" T.J. said, trying to keep the anger from her voice.

"I don't know how I missed. You have a lot of lives, T.J. You're like a cat. But even cats run out of luck, sooner or later." There was pure malice in her eyes.

Joanne freed herself from Hayward's protective embrace. "David will be upset that you found him. He'll be angry with me for hiring you in the first place. I think you should all leave now. He'll be here soon."

The stunned silence in the room was broken by the sound of the doorbell.

"That'll be Marsh," T.J. said. "I called him before I came over here."

* * *

"How did you get all the pieces to fit?" Gregg asked.

"It wasn't hard," T.J. said, "Once I began to ask myself one simple question, the one I'd been ignoring. Why the hell would a man with David Sinclair's background, risk everything, including his life, to be with Joanne? There was only one answer. He wouldn't. The photo you had analyzed was fifteen years old. Why was that the only picture Joanne had of him? Because it was the only photograph that Michael Sinclair had of his camera shy brother. As far as Mrs. McPheron, she never saw David Sinclair; and neither did any of the other household servants. She saw only symbols of Joanne's fantasy. Of course she didn't know it was a fantasy. She saw the props that Joanne used; scattered clothing, dirty dishes and other affects. It was scenery to indicate occupancy of the guest cottage. But the most conclusive, and the most obvious evidence that he didn't exist in Joanne's life, except as a fantasy, was the fact that the police never found one single print belonging to him at the house, because he was never there. Of course, they weren't looking for his prints, either. They believed Joanne had killed him too, and buried him somewhere."

"And she wasn't pregnant?"

"Joanne is sterile. That's what the friendly receptionist told me at her gynecologist's office. And a friendly nurse's aid who'd been on duty both times that Hayward was admitted to emergency, told me that he was held overnight for observation the night Michael died, so he couldn't have killed him."

"Then why did he confess?"

"It was a cleverly devised plan to get the case against Joanne dismissed. It almost worked."

"Besides a feeling, what else convinced you that David Sinclair was nothing more than a fantasy for Joanne?"

"You mean finally? The man himself, when I found him, or, I should say he found me."

* * *

Tim Clancy had left the room quietly. The man he'd introduced as David Sinclair stepped into the center of the room. He looked older than his picture by more than the fifteen years since it had been taken. Still handsome, creases lined his eyes and mouth, and there was a touch of grey at his temples. There was hardness to him, in his face, and in his body. He'd lived a hazardous life, and it showed.

"So, you're David Sinclair," T.J. said. "You've led me a merry chase, you know."

"And all for nothing," he said. "I've been reading my press. It was like reading about someone else. I've never even met Joanne Kirkland."

T.J. smiled. "That was something I figured out before I came here. Why show yourself now?"

"Curiosity. I wanted to meet the woman Tim talked about. You impressed him, and believe me that takes some doing."

"He looked out for you, didn't he?"

David frowned. "He was the only one in my life who ever did. That must seem like a strange statement. He was the man who molded me into what I became, a hired killer."

"And, your brother?"

"At best, we had an arms-length relationship. When he found me about ten years ago, at the company's behest, he was doing what he was best at. He liked the idea of being a spy. It was just another role for him to play." He shook his head. "He didn't have a clue what being a spy entailed. There's nothing glamorous about living a life without friends, trusting no one, afraid to let yourself feel, living sometimes one hour at a time."

"Joanne turned you into a saint, did you know that?"

"I heard."

He was hard, and he was relentless, T.J. acknowledged, and he was by his own admission, a paid killer. Yet, for a brief moment she felt a strange kinship with him. Joanne had used them both. Had cost them both. She had cost her Scott, and Joanne had cost David the risk of discovery.

"What will you do now? Where will you go?" she asked.

"Tim is trying to field me a deal. My life, for a guarantee of permanent amnesia. He means well, but someday I will have a nice convenient accident. I know it, and he knows it, but we play the game anyway." He smiled. "You know what they say, you can run, but you can't hide. I don't even want to anymore."

"Isn't there a chance they'll let you go?"

"There's always a chance. Just like there was always a chance I'd miss my assigned target."

"Did you?"

"Never."

There was no sense of remorse or fear in his voice, just a quiet acceptance of the way things were.

"How many people did you kill?"

"More than I should. More than I wanted to. More than anyone is entitled to."

She extended her hand. He shook it. "You might have liked being the man Joanne made of you. Under different circumstances, you might have been that man."

He grinned. It took some of the hardness out of his eyes. "And God didn't make little green apples. Joanne Kirkland had to live a fantasy. People like you and me don't have that luxury, Miss McCall. Everyday the real world reaches out and threatens to suck us under, but we survive without delusions."

It should have bothered her that he was comparing his existence, his life, to hers, but it didn't, because she understood his logic.

"Good luck, David Sinclair," she said. "I suppose everyone deserves a chance to start over again if they truly regret their mistakes. God knows I made a few of my own."

She turned to leave.

"Did she kill Michael?" he asked.

"Everything points to it."

"What will happen to her?"

He seemed to really care. His concern took her by surprise.

He shrugged. "The lady made me into a good guy."

179

T.J. nodded. "She'll never serve a day in prison. Not a prison as we know it, anyway. She put up her own barred windows a long time ago. She needs help. I'll do my best to see she gets that help."

"That's big of you, considering what happened to your boyfriend."

"It wasn't all her fault. I could have saved him. I should have guessed the truth sooner, or I could have quit. We all have our crosses. That's mine."

Chapter Twenty-Two

Pearl placed the manila folder labeled Joanne Sinclair in the filing cabinet labeled: CLOSED CASES. She slammed the cabinet drawer shut. "It's over, then. Joanne is getting the help she needs, and Hayward is free from murder charges. Odds are, with Jim as his attorney, he'll beat any conspiracy charges. I feel sorry for Hayward. He was the man with everything."

"Everything except a family," T.J. said. "He never married, and he wanted so badly for Joanne to be his daughter. Too bad he'll never know the truth."

"What about blood tests?"

"He won't put her through it."

"Then you feel sorry for him, too?"

"No. And save your pity, he doesn't deserve it."

It was a shade callous for T.J. "You have that look again. What is it? It is over, isn't it? Joanne killed Michael, and she tried to kill you. Her killing Michael Sinclair I can understand, but I wouldn't have thought her capable of hurting you."

"Every move to hurt me was really a cry for help, but nobody was listening, least of all me. The night I was run off the road, she refused sedation. She must have waited for me to leave, and then took off after me. One can only imagine her state of mind. She had moments of true madness."

"Like the night she set fire to your house?"

"I have to believe that." T.J. squeezed Pearl's arm. "Keep a light on in the window. I'll be back."

"Where are you going?"

"To defang a snake," T.J. said.

*　*　*

T.J. was buzzed into Jim's office. He looked up at she entered. "I'm glad you came. If you hadn't come to me, I would have come to you."

She started to interrupt him, but he waved her off. "No, let me finish. For once in your life, let me say what I have to, without cutting me off. I love you, T.J. I never stopped loving you. We proved the other night that we belong together. No two people that good in bed should put up walls. I'll even try to change. I don't promise anything, except that I'll work at making a go of it. What do you say?"

"It's too late, Jim, even if I wanted to try again. We handle sex well. It's a relationship we can't handle. Our breaking up wasn't all your fault."

"I'm sorry about the other women. It was stupid, and it was easy, and at times it was heady. Suddenly, women who wouldn't have given me a second look were ready to sleep with me and all because I was a successful attorney. I took advantage of that. And I took advantage of you."

"I've thought about that a lot lately," T.J. said. "If I'd been enough women for you, you wouldn't have wanted nor needed that kind of high. I don't blame you anymore."

"Then why...?"

"We really are over, Jim. Scott convinced me I deserve better."

He frowned. "Then why are you here?"

Her manner changed. She was no longer conciliatory or understanding. "Business. I came to look you in the eye and to tell you that you're a bigger son of a bitch than I gave you credit for, and I gave you a lot of credit."

"I don't understand. Just now you were...What in the hell did I do to deserve...?"

"You know what you did. Don't make it worse by acting naïve about it. It wasn't a stroke of good luck that Hayward up and 'confessed' to Michael's murder. You two legal giants planned it that way. Things weren't going well after Joanne laid that bombshell in court about being pregnant which, of course, she wasn't. It was merely an extension of her fantasy. You wanted insurance for a victory. You couldn't count on acquittal anymore, so you settled for dismissal. You knew Hayward had a cast iron alibi for Michael Sinclair's murder, because he told you he did. The two of you cooked up a scheme to get the case against Joanne dismissed, with a sure-fire guarantee that Hayward would be cleared of the same charge. You went so far as to get copies of his admittance to emergency the night Michael was killed. When were you going to produce that document? Right after the prosecution looked like it had an open and shut case?"

Jim seemed undecided. He searched her face for a sign of weakness, but unlike a few moments earlier he found none. "Why can't you separate the man from the job, T.J.?" I'm a damned good lawyer. I was being a damned good lawyer when I did everything you've accused me of. What about you? Haven't you ever forgotten to dot an I, cross a T? Underneath, we're not so different, you and I."

"Sadly enough, you believe that. I called a press conference for later today. Maybe what you did won't cost you disbarment, but it will cost you a chance to sit in a judge's seat anytime soon. You know what the worst thing is? A small part of me will always feel something for you, but I can live with that. Goodbye, Jim. Please don't try to see me again."

* * *

The cemetery was almost deserted. Only one other couple tended a plot nearby. T.J. laid her bouquet of red and white roses on Scott's grave.

A gentle hand was placed on her shoulder. "Pearl said I'd find you here," Marshall said.

"Scott was a good man," T.J. said. "All he wanted was to be a credible analyst, to help people, and to spend the rest of his life with me, and that got him killed."

"He was grateful for what little time he had with you. A few precious moments are more than a lot of people ever get."

"I was blessed." She sighed. "Don't worry about me, Marsh, I'm not going to crawl into a shell again. Scott wouldn't have wanted that. I won't say I don't wish things had been different, and that I had more insight. I'm not perfect, Marsh, and I accept that." She attempted a smile. "Life goes on, right?"

"Right. Speaking of not being perfect, you did a number on Westfield. He lost a lot of his present case load, including Hayward."

"He'll get over it. All I did was make his climb to the top a little harder, but he'll get there."

"You and him?" Marshall said. "Hard to figure."

"Not really. Jim was different in the beginning, before ambition and the taste of power changed him."

"Speaking of power, Hayward announced his retirement. Regardless, he says, of how the conspiracy charges against him turn out."

"I heard."

"Well, enough about them. Pearl told me to tell you that you have a new client. Are you ready to go back to work?"

She bent down and placed her fingers on her lips, mouthed a kiss, then caressed the surface of the plate that bore Scott's name. "Goodbye, Scott," she whispered. "I'll always love you."

She stood, linked her arm through Marshall's, and said, " I will be...in time. I think I will take Pearl on a long vacation. She has earned it.."

"And, so My Dear, have you. Where will you go?

"I have not decided. Europe, maybe. I never did really see London,

Off to the right, leaning up against a tree, a cigarette between his lips, a man nodded his head, a look of appreciation in his eyes.

Joanne had touched his life just as she had the red-haired woman detective. Tim Clancy joined David Sinclair.

"You like her," Tim said

"I do. Not that it does me any good. Maybe if...in another lifetime...or..."

Tim frowned. "Don't even go there. She's off limits, and anyway you have a government agency to square yourself with.

"It would be my risk."

"And hers. Come on, let's go. There is nothing here for you."

David ground out his cigarette. You're right...again". One thing he'd learned a long time ago was that you never looked back. You couldn't afford to. He turned to take one last glance at T.J. "Pity, though."

He walked off in the opposite direction to that of T.J. and Marshall, until the distance between them became so great they were like dots on the horizon.

The End

CPSIA information can be obtained
at www.ICGtesting.com
Printed in the USA
BVHW071606141021
618959BV00003B/106